OCTOBER VAGABONDS

RICHARD LE GALLIENNE

October Vagabonds

Richard Le Gallienne

© 1st World Library – Literary Society, 2004
PO Box 2211
Fairfield, IA 52556
www.1stworldlibrary.org
First Edition

LCCN: 2005901378

Softcover ISBN: 1-4218-1180-4
Hardcover ISBN: 1-4218-1080-8
eBook ISBN: 1-4218-1280-0

Purchase *"October Vagabonds"*
as a traditional bound book at:
www.1stWorldLibrary.org/purchase.asp?ISBN=1-4218-1180-4

October Vagabonds
contributed by Tim, Ed & Rodney
in support of
1st World Library Literary Society

CONTENTS

CHAPTER I

THE EPITAPH OF SUMMER

As I started out from the farm with a basket of potatoes, for our supper in the shack half a mile up the hillside, where we had made our Summer camp, my eye fell on a notice affixed to a gate-post, and, as I read it, my heart sank - sank as the sun was sinking yonder with wistful glory behind the purple ridge. I tore the paper from the gate-post and put it in my pocket with a sigh.

"It is true, then," I said to myself. "We have got to admit it. I must show this to Colin."

Then I continued my way across the empty, close-gleaned corn-field, across the railway track, and, plunging into the orchard on the other side, where here and there among the trees the torrents of apples were being already caught in boxes by the thrifty husbandman, began to breast the hill intersected with thickly wooded watercourses.

High up somewhere amid the cloud of beeches and button-wood trees, our log cabin lay hid, in a gully made by the little stream that filled our pails with a silver trickle over a staircase of shelving rock, and up there Colin was already busy with his skilled French cookery, preparing our evening meal. The woods still made a pompous show of leaves, but I knew it to be a hollow sham, a mask of foliage soon to be stripped off by equinoctial fury, a precarious stage-setting, ready to be blown down at the first gusts from the north. A forlorn bird here and there made a thin piping, as it flitted homelessly amid the bleached long grasses, and the frail silk of the milkweed pods came floating along ghostlike on the evening breeze.

Yes! It was true. Summer was beginning to pack up, the great stage-carpenter was about to change the scene, and the great theatre was full of echoes and sighs and sounds of farewell. Of course, we had known it for some time, but had not had the heart to admit it to each other, could not find courage to say that one more golden Summer was at an end. But the paper I had torn from the roadside left us no further shred of illusion. There was an authoritative announcement there was no blinking, a notice to quit there was no gain-saying.

As I came to the crest of the hill, and in sight of the shack, shining with early lamp-light deep down among the trees of the gully, I could see Colin innocently at work on a salad, and hear him humming to himself his eternal "*Vive le Capitaine.*"

It was too pathetic. I believe the tears came to my eyes.

"Colin," I said, as I at length arrived and set down my basket of potatoes, "read this."

He took the paper from my hand and read:

"*Sun-up Baseball Club. September* 19, 1908. *Last Match of the Season*"

He knew what I meant.

"Yes!" he said. "It is the epitaph of Summer."

CHAPTER II

AT EVENING I CAME TO THE WOOD

My solitude had been kindly lent to me for the Summer by a friend, the prophet-proprietor of a certain famous Well of Truth some four miles away, whither souls flocked from all parts of America to drink of the living waters. I had been feeling town-worn and world-weary, and my friend had written me saying: "At Elim are twelve wells and seventy palm-trees," and so to Elim I had betaken myself. After a brief sojourn there, drinking of the waters, and building up on the strong diet of the sage's living words, he had given me the key to some green woods and streams of his, and bade me take them for my hermitage. I had a great making-up to arrange with Nature, and I half wondered how she would receive me after all this long time. But when did that mother ever turn her face from her child, however truant from her care? It had been with a beating heart that I had passed up the hillside on an evening in early June, and approached the hushed green temple, wherein I was to take Summer sanctuary from a wicked world.

But if, as I hope, the reader has no objection to an occasional interlude of verse in all this prose, I will copy for him here the poem I wrote next morning - it being always easier to tell the strict truth in poetry rather than in prose:

At evening I came to the wood, and threw myself on the breast
Of the great green mother, weeping, and the arms of a
thousand trees

Waved and rustled in welcome, and murmured: "Rest - rest - rest!
The leaves, thy brothers, shall heal thee; thy sisters, the flowers,
bring peace."

At length I stayed from my weeping, and lifted my face from the
grass;
The moon was walking the wood with feet of mysterious pearl,
And the great trees held their breath, trance-like, watching her
pass,
And a bird called out from the shadows, with voice as sweet as a
girl.

And then, in the holy silence, to the great green mother I prayed:
"Take me again to thy bosom, thy son who so close to thee,
Aforetime, filial clung, then into the city strayed -
The painted face of the town, the wine and the harlotry.

"Bathe me in lustral dawns, and the morning star and the dew.
Make pure my heart as a bird and innocent as a flower,
Make sweet my thoughts as the meadow-mint
- O make me all anew,
And in the strength of beech and oak gird up my will with power.

"I have wandered far, O my mother, but here I return at the last,
Never again to stray in pilgrimage wanton and wild;
A broken heart and a contrite here at thy feet I cast,
O take me back to thy bosom ..." And the mother answered,
"Child!"

It was a wonderful reconciliation, a wonderful home-coming,
and how I luxuriated in the great green forgiveness! Yes! the
giant maples had forgiven me, and the multitudinous beeches
had taken me to their arms. The flowers and I were friends
again, the grass was my brother, and the shy nymph-like
stream, dropping silver vowels into the silence, was my
sweetheart.

CHAPTER III

"TRESPASSERS WILL BE..."

For those who value it, there is no form of property that inspires a sense of ownership so jealous as solitude. Rob my orchard if you will, but beware how you despoil me of my silence. The average noisy person can have no conception what a brutal form of trespass his coarsely cheerful voice may be in the exquisite spiritual hush of the woods, or what shattering discomfort his irrelevant presence in the landscape.

One day, to my horror, a picnic ruthlessly invaded my sanctuary. With a roar of Boeotian hilarity, it tore up the hillside as if it were a storming party, and half a day the sacred woods were vocal with silly catcalls and snatches of profane song. I locked up my hermitage, and, taking my stick, sought refuge in flight, like the other woodland creatures; only coming back at evening with cautious step and peering glance, half afraid lest it should still be there. No! It was gone, but its voices seemed to have left gaping wounds across the violated air, and the trees to wear a look of desecration. But presently the moon arose and washed the solitude clean again, and the wounds of silence were healed in the still night.

Next morning I amused myself by writing the following notice, which I nailed up on a great elm-tree standing guard at the beginning of the woods:

SILENCE!

Speaking above a whisper in these woods
is forbidden by law.

This notice seems to have had its effect, for from this time on no more hands of marauders invaded my peace. But I had one other case of trespass, of which it is now time to speak.

Some short distance from the shack was a clearing in the woods, a thriving wilderness of bramble-bushes, poke-berries, myrtle-berries, mandrakes, milkweed, mullein, daisies and what not - a paradise of every sauntering vine and splendid, saucy weed. In the centre stood a sycamore-tree, beneath which it was my custom to smoke a morning pipe and revolve my profound after-breakfast thoughts.

Judge, then, of my indignant shock, one morning, at finding a stranger calmly occupying my place. I stood for a moment rooted to the spot, in the shadow of the encircling woods, and he had not yet seen me. As I stood, pondering on the best way of dealing with the intruder, a sudden revulsion of kindness stole over me. For here indeed was a very different figure from what, in my first shock of surprise, I had expected to see. No common intruder this. In fact, who could have dreamed of coming upon so incongruous an apparition as this in an American woodland? How on earth did this picturesque waif from the Quartier Latin come to stray so far away from the Boul' Miche! For the little boyish figure of a man that sat sketching in my place was the Frenchiest-looking Frenchman you ever saw - with his dark, smoke-dried skin, his long, straight, blue-black hair, his fine, rather ferocious brown eyes, his long, delicate French nose, his bristling black moustache and short, sting-shaped imperial. He wore on his head a soft white felt hat, somewhat of the shape affected by circus clowns, and too small for him. His coat was of green velveteen corduroy and he wore knickerbockers of an eloquent plaid.

He was intently absorbed in sketching a prosperous group of weeds, a crazy quilt of wildly jostling colour, that had grown up around the decay of a fallen tree, and made a fine blazon of

RICHARD LE GALLIENNE

contrast against the massed foliage in the background. There was no mistake how the stranger loved this patch of coloured weeds. Here was a man whose whole soul was evidently - colour. There was a look in his face as if he could just eat those oranges and purples, and soft greens; and there was a sort of passionate assurance in the way in which he handled his brushes, and delicately plunged them here and there in his colour-box, that spoke a master. So intent was he upon his work that, when I came up behind him, he seemed unaware of my presence; though his oblivion was actually the conscious indifference of a landscape painter, accustomed to the ambling cow and the awe-struck peasant looking over his shoulder as he worked.

"Great bunch of weeds," he said presently, without looking up, and still painting, drawing the while at a quaint pipe about an inch long.

"O, you are not the Boul' Miche, after all," I exclaimed in disappointment.

"Aren't I, though?" he said at last, looking up in interested surprise. "Ever at -?" mentioning the name of a well-known cafe, one of the many rally-points of the Quartier.

"I should say," I answered.

"Well!"

And thereupon we both plunged into delighted reminiscence of that city which, as none other, makes immediate friends of all her lovers. For a while the woods faded away, and in that tangled clearing rose the towers of Notre Dame, and the Seine glittered on under its great bridges, and again the world smelled of absinthe, and picturesque madmen gesticulated in clouds of tobacco smoke, and propounded fantastic philo-sophies amid the rattle of dominoes - and afar off in the street a voice was crying "*Haricots verts*!" My new friend's talk had the pathos of spiritual exile, for, as French in blood as a man could be, born in Bordeaux of Provencal parentage, he had lived most of his life in America. The decoration of a rich man's house in the neighbourhood had brought him thus into my solitude, and, that work completed, he would return to his home in New York.

Meanwhile the morning was going by as we talked, and, putting up his sketch-box, he accepted my invitation to join me at lunch.

Such was the manner of my meeting, in the guise of a trespasser, with the dear friend to whom I had brought the decisive news of the death of Summer, as he was innocently making a salad, *in antiquam silvam*, on that sad September evening.

CHAPTER IV

SALAD AND MOONSHINE

"Do you remember that first salad you made us, Colin?" I said, as we sat over our coffee, and Colin was filling his little pipe. "A daring work of art, a fantastic *tour de force*, of apples, and lettuce, and wild strawberries, and I don't know what else."

"I believe I mixed in some May-apples, too. It was a great stunt ... well, no more May-apples and strawberries this year," he finished, with a sigh, and we both sat silently smoking, thinking over the good Summer that was gone.

After our first meeting, Colin had dropped in to see me again from time to time, and when his work at the great house was finished, I had asked him to come and share my solitude. A veritable child of Nature himself, he fitted into my quiet days as silently as a squirrel. So much of his life had been passed out-of-doors with trees and skies, long dream-like days all alone sketching in solitary places, that he seemed as much a part of the woods as though he were a faun, and the lore of the elements, and all natural things - bugs and birds, all wildwood creatures - had passed into him with unconscious absorption. A sort of boyish unconsciousness, indeed, was the keynote and charm of his nature. A less sophisticated creature never followed the mystic calling of art. Fortunately for me, he was not one of those painters who understand and expound their own work. On the contrary, he was a perfect child about it, and painted for no more mysterious reason than that his eye delighted in beautiful natural effects, and that he loved to play with paint and brushes. Though he was undoubtedly sensitive somewhere to the mystic side of Nature, her Wordsworthian "intimations," you would hardly have guessed it from his talk. "A bully bit of colour," would be his craftsmanlike way of describing a twilight full of sibylline suggestiveness to the literary mind. But, strangely enough, when he brought you his sketch, all your "sibylline suggestiveness" was there, which of course means, after all, that painting was his way of seeing and saying it.

The moon rose as we smoked on, and began to lattice with silver the darkness of the glen, and flood the hillside with misty radiance. Colin made for his sketch-box.

"I must make good use of this moon," he said, "before we go."

"And so must I," said I, laughing as we both went out into the night, he one way and I another, to make our different uses of the moon.

An hour later Colin turned in with a panel that seemed made of moonlight. "How on earth did you do it?" I said. "It is as though you had drawn up the moon in a silver bucket from the bottom of a fairy well."

"No, no," he protested; "I know better. But where is your *clair de lune*?"

"Nothing doing," I answered.

"Well, then, say those lines you wrote a week or two ago instead."

"'Berries already,' do you mean?"

"Yes."

Here are the lines he meant:

Berries already, September soon, -
The shortening day and like early moon;
The year is busy with next year's flowers
The seeds are ready for next year' showers;
Through a thousand tossing trees there swells
The sigh of the Summer's sad farewells.
Too soon those leaves in the sunset sky
Low down on the wintry ground will lie,
And grim November and December
Leave naught of Summer to remember -
Saving some flower in a book put by,
Secure from the soft effacing snow,
Though all the rest of the Summer go.

CHAPTER V

THE GREEN FRIEND

Though we had received such unmistakable notice to quit, we still lingered on in our solitude, after the manner of defiant tenants whom nothing short of corporal ejection can dislodge. The North wind began to roar in the tree-tops and shake the doors and windows of the shack, like an angry landlord, but we paid no heed to him. Yet, all the time, both of us, in our several ways, were saying our farewells, and packing up our memories for departure. There was an old elm-tree which Colin had taken for his Summer god, and which he was never tired of painting. He must make the one perfect study of that before we pulled up stakes. So, each day, after our morning adoration of the sun, we would separate about our different ways and business.

The woods were already beginning to wear a wistful, dejected look. There was a feeling of departure everywhere, a sense that the year's excitements were over. The procession had gone by, and there was an empty, purposeless air of waiting-about upon things, a sort of despairing longing for something else to happen - and a sure sense that nothing more could happen till next year. Every event in the floral calendar had taken place with immemorial punctuality and tragic rapidity. All the full-blooded flowers of Summer had long since come and gone, with their magic faces and their souls of perfume. Gone were the banners of blossom from the great trees. The locust and the chestnut, those spendthrifts of the woods, that went the pace so gorgeously in June, are now sober-coated enough, and

RICHARD LE GALLIENNE

growing even threadbare. All the hum and the honey and breathless bosom-beat of things is over. The birds sing no more, but only chatter about time-tables. The bee keeps to his hive, and the bewildered butterfly, in tattered ball-dress, wonders what has become of his flowery partners. The great cricket factory has shut down. Not a wheel is heard whirring. The squirrel has lost his playful air, and has an anxious manner, as though there were no time to waste before stocking his granary. Everywhere berries have taken the place of buds, and bearded grasses the place of flowers. Even the goldenrod has fallen to rust, and the stars of the aster are already tarnished. Only along the edges of the wood the dry little paper immortelles spread long shrouds and wreaths in the shade.

Suddenly you feel lonely in the woods, which had seemed so companionable all Summer. What is it - *Who* is it - that has gone? Though quite alone, there was some one with you all Summer, an invisible being filling the woods with his presence, and always at your side, or somewhere near by. But to-day, through all the green halls and chambers of the wood, you seek him in vain. You call, but there is no answer. You wait, but he does not come. He has gone. The wood is an empty palace. The prince went away secretly in the night. The wood is a deserted temple. The god has betaken himself to some secret abode. Everywhere you come upon chill, abandoned altars, littered debris of Summer sacrifices. Maybe he is dead, and perchance, deeper in the wood, you may come upon his marble form in a winding-sheet of drifting leaves.

Not a god, maybe, you have pictured him, not a prince, but surely as a friend - the mysterious Green Friend of the green silence and the golden hush of Summer noons. The mysterious Green Friend of the woods! So strangely by our side all Summer, so strangely gone away. It is in vain to await him under our morning sycamore, nor under the great maples shall we find him walking, nor amid the alder thickets discover him, nor yet in the little ravine beneath the pines. No! he has surely gone away, and his great house seems empty without him, desolate, filled with lamentation, all its doors and windows open to the Winter snows.

But the Green Friend had left me a message. I found it at the roots of some violets. "*I shall be back again next year*" he said.

RICHARD LE GALLIENNE

CHAPTER VI

IN THE WAKE OF SUMMER

Yes, it was time to be going, and the thought was much on both our minds. We had as yet, however, made no plans, had not indeed discussed any; but one afternoon, late in September, driven indoors by a sudden squall of rain, I came to Colin with an idea. The night before we had had the first real storm of the season.

"Ah! This will do their business," Colin had said, referring to the trees, as we heard the wind and rain tearing and splashing through the pitch-dark woods. "It will be a different world in the morning."

And indeed it was. Cruel was the work of dismantling that had gone on during the night. The roof of the wood had fallen in in a score of places, letting in the sky through unfamiliar windows; and the distant prospect showed through the torn tapestry of the trees with a startling sense of disclosure. The dishevelled world wore the distressed look of a nymph caught *deshabillee.* The expression, "the naked woods," occurred to one with almost a sense of impropriety. At least there was a cynical indecorum in this violent disrobing of the landscape.

"Colin," I said, coming to him with my idea. "We've got to go, of course, but I've been thinking - don't you hate the idea of being hurled along in a train, and suddenly shot into the city again, like a package through a tube?"

"Hate it? Don't ask me," said Colin.

"If only it could be more gradual," I went on. "Suppose, for instance, instead of taking the train, we should walk it!"

"Walk to New York?" said Colin, with a surprised whistle.

"Yes! Why not?"

"Something of a walk, old man."

"All the better. We shall be all the longer getting there. But, listen. To go by train would be almost too sudden a shock. I don't believe we could stand it. To be here to-day, breathing this God's fresh air, living the lives of natural men in a natural world, and to-morrow - Broadway, the horrible crowds, the hustle, the dirt, the smells, the uproar."

For answer Colin watched the clean rain fleeting through the trees, and groaned aloud.

"But now if we walked, we would, so to say, let ourselves down lightly, inure ourselves by gradual approach to the thought of life once more with our fellows. Besides, we should be walking in the wake of the Summer. She has only moved a little East as yet. We might catch her up on her way to New York, and thus move with the moving season, keeping in step with the Zodiac. Then, at last, ... how much more fitting our entry into New York, not by way of some sordid and clangorous depot, but through the spacious corridors of the Highlands and the lordly gates of the Hudson!"

When I had thus attained my crescendo, Colin rose impressively, and embraced me with true French effusion.

"Old man," he said, "that's just great. It's an inspiration from on high. It makes me feel better already. Gee! but that's bully."

French as was his blood, it will be observed that Colin's

expletives were thoroughly American. Of course, he should have said *sacre mille cochons* or *nom de Dieu de nom de Dieu*; but, though in appearance, so to say, an embodied *"sacre"* he seemed to find the American vernacular sufficiently expressive.

"Is it a go, then?" said I.

"It's a go," said Colin, once more in American.

And we shook on it.

CHAPTER VII

MAPS AND FAREWELLS

It was wonderful what a change our new plan wrought in our spirits.

Our melancholy was immediately dispersed, and its place taken by active anticipations of our journey. The North wind in the trees, instead of blustering dismissal, sounded to our ears like the fluttering of the blue-peter at the masthead of our voyage. Strange heart of man! A day back we were in tears at the thought of going. Now we are all smiles to think of it, all impatience to be gone. We quote Whitman a dozen times in the hour, and it is all "afoot and light-hearted" with us, and "the open road."

But there were some farewells to make to people as well as to trees. There were friends at Elim to bid adieu, and also there were maps to be consulted, and knapsacks to be packed - exhilarating preparations.

Our friends looked at us, when we had unfolded our project, with a mixture of surprise and pity. "Amiable lunatics" was the first comment of their countenances, and - "There never was any telling what the artistic temperament would do next!" Had we announced an air-ship voyage to the moon, they would have regarded us as comparatively reasonable, but to walk - *to walk* - some four or five hundred miles in America, of all countries, a country of palace cars and, lightning limited expresses, not to mention homicidal touring automobiles,

RICHARD LE GALLIENNE

seemed like - what shall I say? - well, as though one should start out for New Zealand in a row-boat, or make the trip to St. Petersburg in a sedan-chair.

But there were others - especially the women - who understood, felt as we did, and longed to go with us. I have never met a woman yet whose face did not light up at the thought of a walking tour, and in her heart long to don Rosalind clothes and set forth in search of adventures. We thus had the advantage, in planning our route, of several prettily coiffed heads bending over our maps and guide-books with us.

"Four hundred and thirty miles," said one of these Rosalinds, whose pretty head was full of pictures of romantic European travel. "Think what one could do with four hundred and thirty miles in Europe. Let us try, for the fun of it."

And turning to a map of Europe, and measuring out four hundred and thirty miles by scale on a slip of paper, she tried it up and down the map from point to point. "Look at funny little England!" she said. "Why, you will practically be walking from one end of England to the other. See," and she fitted her scale to the map, "it would bring you easily from Portsmouth to Aberdeen.

"And now let us try France. Why, see again - you will be walking from Calais to Marseilles - think of it! walking through France, all vineyards and beautiful names. Now Italy - see! you will be walking from Florence to Mount Etna - Florence, Rome, Naples, Palermo."

And so in imagination our fair friend sketched out fanciful pilgrimages for us. "You could walk from Gibraltar to the Pyrenees," she went on. "You could walk from Venice to Berlin; from Brussels to Copenhagen; you could walk from Munich to Budapest; you could walk right across Turkey, from Constantinople to the Adriatic Sea. And Greece - see! you could walk from Sparta to the Danube. To think of the romantic use you could make of your four-hundred-odd-miles, and how different it sounds - Buffalo to New York!"

And again she repeated, luxuriating in the romantic sound of the words: "Constantinople to the Adriatic! Sparta to the Danube! - Buffalo to New York!"

There was not wanting to the party the whole-souled, my-country-'tis-of-thee American, who somewhat resented these European comparisons, and declared that America was good enough for her, clearly intimating that a certain lack of patriotism, even a certain immorality, attached to the admiration of foreign countries. She also told us somewhat severely that the same stars, if not better, shone over America as over any other country, and that American scenery was the finest in the world - not to speak of the American climate.

To all of which we bowed our heads in silence - but the frivolous, European-minded Rosalind who had got us into this trouble retorted with a grave face: "Wouldn't you just love, dear Miss -, to walk from Hackensack to Omaha?"

Another voice was kind enough to explain for our encouragement that the traveller found in a place exactly what he brought there, and that romance was a personal gift, all in the personal point of view.

"A sort of cosmetic you apply to the face of Nature," footnoted our irrepressible friend.

Still another reminded us that "to travel hopefully is a better thing than to arrive," and still another strongly advised us to carry revolvers.

So, taking with us our maps and much good advice, we bade farewell to our friends, and walked back to our camp under the stars - the same stars that were shining over Constantinople.

The next day, when all our preparations were complete, the shack swept and garnished, and our knapsacks bulging in readiness for the road, Colin took his brushes, and in a few minutes had decorated one of the walls with an Autumn sunset - a sort of memorial tablet to our Summer, he explained.

"Can't you think up a verse to put underneath?" he asked.

Then underneath he lettered:

> *Two lovers of the Sun and of the Moon,*
> *Lovers of Tree and Grass and Bug and Bird,*
> *Spent here the Summer days, then all too soon*
> *Upon the homeward track reluctant fared.*

> *Sun-up, October 1, 1908.*

Some apples remained over from our larder. We carefully laid them outside for the squirrels; then, slinging our knapsacks, we took a last look round the little place, and locked the door.

Our way lay up the hill, across the pasture and through the beeches, toward the sky-line.

We stood still a moment, gazing at the well-loved landscape. Then we turned and breasted the hill.

"*Allons!*" cried Colin.

"*Allons!*" I answered. "*Allons!* To New York!"

CHAPTER VIII

THE AMERICAN BLUEBIRD AND ITS SONG

I wish I could convey the singular feeling of freedom and adventure that possessed us as Colin and I grasped our sticks and struck up the green hill - for New York. It was a feeling of exhilaration and romantic expectancy, blent with an absurd sense of our being entirely on our own resources, vagrants shifting for ourselves, independent of civilization; which, of course, the actual circumstances in no way warranted. A delightful boyish illusion of entering on untrodden paths and facing unknown dangers thrilled through us.

"Well, we're off!" we said simultaneously, smiling interrogatively at each other.

"Yes! we're in for it."

So men start out manfully for the North Pole.

Our little enterprise gave us an imaginative realization of the solidarity, the interdependence, of the world; and we saw, as in a vision, its four corners knit together by a vast network of paths connecting one with the other; footpaths, byways, cart-tracks, bride-paths, lovers' lanes, highroads, all sensitively linked in one vast nervous system of human communication. This field whose green sod we were treading connected with another field, that with another, and that again with another - all the way to New York - all the way to Cape Horn! No break anywhere. All we had to do was to go on putting one foot before the other, and we could arrive anywhere. So the worn old phrase, "All roads lead to Rome," lit up with a new meaning, the meaning that had originally made it. Yes! the loneliest of lovers' lanes, all silence and wild flowers, was on the way to the Metropolitan Opera House; or, vice versa, the Flat Iron Building was on the way to the depths of the forest.

"Suppose we stop here, Colin," I said, pointing to a solitary, forgotten-looking little farmhouse, surrounded by giant wind-worn poplars that looked older than America, "and ask the way to Versailles?"

"And I shouldn't be surprised," answered Colin, "if we struck some bright little American schoolgirl who could tell us."

Although we as yet knew every foot of the ground we were treading, it already began to wear an unfamiliar houseless and homeless look, an air of foreign travel, and though the shack was but a few yards behind us, it seemed already miles away, wrapped in lonely distance, wistfully forsaken. Everything we looked at seemed to have gained a new importance and significance; every tree and bush seemed to say, "So many miles to New York," and we unconsciously looked at and remarked on the most trifling objects with the eye of explorers, and took as minute an interest in the usual bird and wayside weed as though we were engaged in some "flora and fauna" survey of untrodden regions.

"That's a bluebird," said Colin, as a faint pee-weeing came with a thin melancholy note from a telegraph wire. And we both listened attentively, with a learned air, as though making a mental note for some ornithological society in New York. "Bluebird seen in Erie County, October 1, 1908!" So might Sir John Mandeville have noted the occurrence of birds of paradise in the domains of Prester John.

"That's a silo," said Colin, pointing to a cylindrical tower at the end of a group of barns, from which came the sound of an engine surrounded by a group of men, occupied in feeding it with trusses of corn from a high-piled wagon. "They are laying in fodder for the Winter." Interesting agricultural observation!

In the surrounding fields the pumpkins, globes of golden orange, lay scattered among the wintry-looking corn-stalks.

"Bully subject for a picture!" said Colin.

Before we had gone very far, we did stop at a cottage standing at a puzzling corner of cross-roads, and asked the way, not to Versailles, indeed, but to - Dutch Hollow. We were answered by a good-humoured German voice belonging to an old dame, who seemed glad to have the lonely afternoon silence broken by human speech; and we were then, as often after-ward, reminded that we were not so far away from Europe, after all; but that, indeed, in no small degree the American continent was the map of Europe bodily transported across the sea. For the present our way lay through Germany.

Dutch Hollow! The name told its own story, and it had appealed to our imaginations as we had come upon it on the map.

We had thought we should like to see how it looked written in trees and rocks and human habitations on the page of the landscape. And I may say that it was such fanciful considerations as this, rather than any more business-like manner of travel, that frequently determined the route of our essentially sentimental journey. If our way admitted of a choice of direction, we usually decided by the sound of the name of village or town. Thus the sound of "Wales Center" had taken us, we were told, a mile or two out of our way; but what of that? We were not walking for a record, nor were we road-surveying, or following the automobile route to New York. In fact, we had deliberately avoided the gasoline route, choosing to be led by more rustic odours; and thus our wayward wayfaring cannot be offered in any sense as a guide for pedestrians who may come after us. Any one following our guidance would be as liable to arrive at the moon as at New

York. In fact, we not infrequently inquired our way of a bird, or some friendly little dog that would come out to bark a companionable good day to us from a wayside porch.

As a matter of fact, I had inquired the way of the bluebird mentioned a little while back, and it may be of interest - to ornithological societies - to transcribe his answer:

The way of dreams - the bluebird sang -
Is never hard to find
So soon as you have really left
The grown-up world behind;

So soon as you have come to see
That what the others call
Realities, for such as you,
Are never real at all;

So soon as you have ceased to care
What others say or do,
And understand that they are they,
And you - thank God - are you.

Then is your foot upon the path,
Your journey well begun,
And safe the road for you to tread,
Moonlight or morning sun.

Pence of this world you shall not take,
Yea! no provision heed;
A wild-rose gathered in the wood
Will buy you all you need.

Hungry, the birds shall bring you food,
The bees their honey bring;
And, thirsty, you the crystal drink
Of an immortal spring

For sleep, behold how deep and soft
With moss the earth is spread,
And all the trees of all the world
Shall curtain round your bed.

Enchanted journey! that begins
Nowhere, and nowhere ends,
Seeking an ever-changing goal,
Nowhither winds and wends.

For destination yonder flower,
For business yonder bird;
Aught better worth the travelling to
I never saw or heard.

O long dream-travel of the soul!
First the green earth to tread -
And still yon other starry track
To travel when you're dead.

CHAPTER IX

DUTCH HOLLOW

The day had opened with a restless picturesque morning of gusty sunshine and rolling clouds. There was something rich and stormy and ominous in the air, and a soft rainy sense of solemn impending change, at once brilliant and mournful; a curious sense of intermingled death and birth, as of withered leaves and dreaming seeds being blown about together on their errands of decay and resurrection by the same breath of the unseen creative spirit. Incidentally it meant a rain-storm by evening, and its mysterious presage had prompted Colin to the furnishing of our knapsacks with water-proof cloaks, which, as the afternoon wore on, seemed more and more a wise provision. But the rain still held off, contenting itself with threatening phantasmagoria of cloud, moulding and massing like visible thunder in our wake. It seemed leisurely certain, however, of catching us before nightfall; and, sure enough, as the light began to thicken, and we stood admiring its mountainous magnificence - vast billows of plum-coloured gloom, hanging like doomsday over a stretch of haunted orchard - the great drops began to patter down.

Surely the sky is the greatest of all melodramatists. Nothing short of the cataclysmal end of the world could have provided drama to match the stupendous stage-setting of that stormy sky. All doom and destiny and wrath of avenging deities and days of judgment seemed concentrated in that frown of gigantic darkness. Beneath it the landscape seemed to grow livid as a corpse, and terror to fill with trembling the very trees and grasses. Oedipus and Orestes and King Lear rolled into one could hardly have accounted for that angry sky. Such a sky it must have been that carried doom to the cities of the plain. And, after all, it was only Colin and I innocently making haste to Dutch Hollow!

That Teutonic spot seemed hopelessly far away as the rain began to drive down and the horizon to open here and there in lurid slashings of stormy sunset; and when the road, which for some time had been one long descent, suddenly confronted us with a rough, perpendicular lane, overgrown with bushes, that seemed more like a cart-track to the stars than a sensible thoroughfare, we realized, with a certain indignant self-pity, that we were walking in real earnest, out in the night and the storm, far from human habitation.

"Nature cannot be so absurd," said I, "as to expect us to climb such a road on such an evening! She must surely have placed a comfortable inn in such a place as this, with ruddy windows of welcome, and a roaring fire and a hissing roast." But, alas! our eyes scanned the streaming copses in vain - nothing in sight but trees, rain and a solitary saw-mill, where an old man on a ladder assured us in a broken singsong, like the Scandinavian of the Middle West, that indeed Nature did mean us to climb that hill, and that by that road only could we reach the Promised Land of supper and bed.

And the rain fell and the wind blew, and Colin and I trudged on through the murk and the mire, I silently recalling and commenting on certain passages in certain modern writers in praise of walking in the rain. At last the hill came to an end - we learned afterward that it was a good mile high - and we stumbled out on to some upland wilderness, unlit by star or window. Then we found ourselves descending again, and at last dim shapes of clustered houses began to appear, and the white phantom of a church. We could rather feel than see the houses, for the night was so dark, and, though here was evidently a village, there was no sign of a light anywhere, not so much as a bright keyhole; nothing but hushed, shuttered shapes of deeper black in the general darkness. So English villages must have looked, muffled up in darkness, at the sound of the Conqueror's curfew.

"Surely, they can't all be in bed by seven o'clock?" I said.

"There doesn't seem much to stay up for," laughed Colin.

At length we suspected, rather than saw, a gleam of light at the rear of one of the shrouded shapes we took for houses, and, stumbling toward it, we heard cheerful voices, German voices; and, knocking at a back door, received a friendly summons to enter. Then, out of the night that covered us, suddenly sprang a kitchen full of light and a family at supper, kind German folk, the old people, the younger married couple, and the grandchildren, and a big dog vociferously taking care of them. A lighted glimpse, a few hearty words of direction, and we were out in the night again; for though, indeed, this was Dutch Hollow, its simple microcosm did not include an hotel. For that we must walk on another half-mile or so. O those country half-miles! So on we went again, and soon a lighted stoop flashed on our right. At last! I mounted the steps of a veranda, and, before knocking, looked in at the window. Then I didn't knock, but softly called Colin, who was waiting in the road, and together we looked in. At a table in the centre of a barely furnished, brightly-lit room, an old woman and a young man were kneeling in prayer. Colin and I stood a moment looking at them, and then softly took the road again.

But the inn, or rather the "hotel," did come at last. Alas! however, for dreams of ruddy welcome - rubicund host, and capon turning on the spit. In spite of German accents, we were walking in America, after all. A shabbily-lit glass door admitted us into a dreary saloon bar, where a hard-featured, gruff-mannered young countryman, after serving beer to two farm-labourers, admitted with apparent reluctance that beds were to be had by such as had "the price," but that, as to supper, well! supper was "over" - supper-time was six-thirty; it was now seven-thirty. The young man seemed no little surprised, even indignant, that any one should be ignorant of the fact that supper-time at Sheldon Center was half-past six; and this, by the way, was a surprise we encountered more than once on our journey. Supper-time in the American road-house is an hour severely observed, and you disregard it at the peril of your empty stomach, for no larders seem so hermetically sealed as the larders of American country hotels after the appointed hour, and no favour so impossible to grant as even a ham sandwich, if you should be so much a stranger to local ordinances as to expect it after the striking of the hour. Indeed, you are looked on with suspicion for asking, as something of a tramp or dangerous character. Not to know that supper-time at Sheldon Center was half-past six seemed to argue a sinister disregard of the usages of civilization.

As we ruefully contemplated a supperless couch, a comely young woman, who had been looking us over from a room in the rear of the bar, came smilingly forward and volunteered to do the best she could for us. She was evidently the rough fellow's wife, goddess of the kitchen, and final court of appeal. What a difference a good-natured, good-looking woman makes in a place! 'Tis a glimpse into the obvious, but there are occasions on which such commonplaces shine with a blessed radiance, and the moment when our attractive hostess flowered out upon us from her forbidding background was one of them. With her on our side, we forgot our fears, and, with an assured air, asked her husband to show us to our rooms. Lamp in hand, he led us up staircases and along corridors - for the hotel was quite a barracks - thawing out into conversation on the way. The place, he explained, was a little out of order, owing to "the ball" - an event he referred to as a matter of national knowledge, and being, we understood, the annual ball of harvesting. The fact of the lamps not burning properly, and there being no water or towels in our rooms, was due, he explained, to this disorganizing festival; as also the circumstance of our doors having no knobs to them. "The young fellows at the ball did carry on so," he said, chuckling with reminiscence of that orgiastic occasion. The Sheldon Center gallants were evidently the very devil; and those vanished door-knobs provoked pictures in our minds of Lupercalian revels, which, alas! we had come too late to share.

We should have found anything good that our hostess cared to set before us - so potent a charm is amiability - and I am sure no man need wish for a better supper than the fried eggs and fried potatoes which copiously awaited us down-stairs. As Colin washed his down with coffee, like a true Franco-American, and I washed down mine with English breakfast tea, we pulled out our pipes and smiled contentment at each other.

"Shall we have a chapter of the wisdom of Paragot before bed?" I said, and, going to our small, carefully selected knap-sack library, I found the gay-hearted fantastical book we had promised to read together on our wayfaring; and so the day drew to a good end.

Over the head of my bed hung a highly-coloured reproduction of Leonardo's "Last Supper," and stuck in its frame was a leaf of blessed palm - by which tokens I realized that my slumbers were to be under the wing of the ancient Mother. As I closed my eyes, the musical chime of a great bell, high up somewhere in the outer night, fell in benediction upon the darkness. So I fell asleep in Europe, after all.

CHAPTER X

WHERE THEY SING FROM
MORNING TILL NIGHT

I awoke to the same silvery salutation, and the sound of country boots echoing across farm-yard cobble-stones. A lantern flashing in and out among barns lit up my ceiling for a moment, a rough country voice hailed another rough country voice somewhere outside, and the day slowly coughed and sneezed itself awake in the six-o'clock grayness. I heard Colin moving in the next room, and presently we were down-stairs, alertly hungry. Our hostess, with morning smile, asked if we would mind waiting breakfast for "the boarders." Meanwhile, we stepped out into the unfolding day, and the village that had been a mystery to us in the darkness was revealed; a handful of farmhouses on the brow of a solitary-looking upland, and, looming over all, a great cathedral-like church that seemed to have been transported bodily from France. Stepping out to say good-morning to some young pigs that were sociably grunting in a neighbouring sty, we beheld the vast landscape of our preceding day stretched out beneath us, mistily emerging into the widening sunrise. With pride our eyes traced the steep white road we had so arduously travelled, and, for remembrance, Colin made a swift sketch of Dutch Hollow huddled down there in the valley, with its white church steeple catching the morning sun. And, by this, "the boarders" had assembled, and we found ourselves at breakfast in a cheery company of three workmen, who were as bright and full of fun as boys out for a holiday. They were presently joined by a fourth, a hearty, middle-aged man, who, as he sat down, greeted us with:

"I feel just like singing this morning."

"Good for you!" said one of us. "That's the way to begin the day." His good nature was magnetic.

"Yes," he laughed, "we sing in Sheldon from morning till night."

"Sheldon's evidently a good place to know," I said. "I will make a note of that for New Yorkers."

So, reader, sometimes when the world seems all wrong, and life a very doubtful speculation, you may care to know of a place where the days go so blithely that men actually sing from morning till night! Sheldon Center is that place. You can find it on any map, and I can testify that the news is true.

And the men that thus sang from morning till night - what was the trade they worked and sang at?

We gathered from a few dropped words that they were engaged on some work over at the church - masonry, no doubt - and, as they left the breakfast-table, in a laughing knot, to begin the day's work, they suggested our giving a look in at them on our way. This we promised to do, for a merrier, better-hearted lot of fellows it would be hard to find. To meet them was to feel a warm glow of human comrade-ship. Healthy, normal, happy fellows, enjoying their work as men should, and taking life as it came with sane, unconscious gusto; it was a tonic encounter to be in their company.

They were grave-diggers, engaged in renovating the village churchyard!

Yes! and, said our hostess, they were making it like a garden! It had been long neglected and become disgracefully over-grown with weeds and bushes, but now they were trimming it up in fine style. They were cemetery experts from Batavia way, and the job was to cost sixteen hundred dollars. But it was worth it, for indeed they were making it look like a garden!

Presently we stepped over to the churchyard. We should not have been human if we had not advanced with a Hamlet-Horatio air: "Has this fellow no feeling of his business, that he sings at grave-making?" We found our four friends in a space of the churchyard from which the tombstones had been temporarily removed, engaged, not with mattock and death's head, but with spirit-level and measuring-cord. They were levelling a stretch of newly-turned and smoothed ground, and they pointed with pride to the portion of the work already accomplished, serried rows of spick-and-span headstones, all "plumb," as they explained, and freshly scraped - not a sign of caressing moss or a tendril of vine to be seen. A neat job, if there ever was one. We should have seen the yard before they had taken it in hand! There wasn't a stone that was straight, and the weeds and the brambles - well, look at it now. We looked. Could anything be more refined or in more perfect taste? The churchyard was as smooth and correct as a newly-barbered head, not a hair out of place. We looked and kept our thoughts to ourselves, but we wondered if the dead were really as grateful as they should be for this drastic house-cleaning? Did they appreciate this mathematical uniformity, this spruce and spotless residential air of their numbered rectangular rest; or was not the old way nearer to their desire, with soft mosses tucking them in from the garish sun, and Spring winds spreading coverlets of wild flowers above their sleep?

But - who knows? - perhaps the dead prefer to be up-to-date, and to follow the fashion in funeral furnishings; and surely such expert necropolitans as our four friends ought to know. No doubt the Sheldon Center dead would have the same tastes as the Sheldon Center living; for, after all, we forget, in our idealization of them, that the dead, like the living, are a vast *bourgeoisie*. Yes! it is a depressing thought - the *bourgeoisie* of the dead!

As we stood talking, the young priest of the parish joined our group. He was a German, from Duesseldorf, and his worn face lit up when he found that Colin had been at Duesseldorf and could talk with him about it. As he stood with us there on that bleak upland, he seemed a pathetic, symbolic figure, lonely standard-bearer of the spirit in one of the dreary colonies of that indomitable church that carries her mystic sacraments even into the waste places and borders of the world. The romance of Rome was far away beyond that horizon on which he turned his wistful look; here was its hard work, its daily prose. But he turned proudly to the great pile that loomed over us. We had commented on its size in so remote a parish.

"Yes, I am proud of our people," he said. "It is greatly to their credit." One could not help silently wondering that the spiritual needs of this handful of lonely houses should demand so ambitious a structure. But the symbols of the soul can never be too impressive. Then we said good-bye to our friends, and struck out into the morning sunshine, leaving the village of song behind.

Yes! in Sheldon Center they sing from morning till night - at grave-making!

CHAPTER XI

APPLE-LAND

It was a spacious morning of windswept sunshine, with a wintry bite in the keen air. Meadow-larks and song-sparrows kept up a faint warbling about us, but the crickets, which yesterday had here and there made a thin music, as of straggling bands of survivors of the Summer, were numbed into silence again. Once or twice we caught sight of the dainty snipe in the meadows, and high over the woods a bird-hawk floated, as by some invisible anchorage, in the sky. It was an austere landscape, grave with elm and ash and pine. For a space, a field of buckwheat standing in ricks struck a smudged negroid note, but there was warmth in the apple orchards which clustered about the scattered houses, with piles of golden pumpkins and red apples under the trees. And is there any form of piled-up wealth, bins of specie at the bank, or mountains of precious stones, rubies and sapphires and carbuncles, as we picture them in the subterranean treasuries of kings, that thrills the imagination with so dream-like a sense of uncounted riches, untold gold, as such natural bullion of the earth; pyramids of apples lighting up dark orchards, great plums lying in heaps of careless purple, corridors hung with fabulous bunches of grapes, or billowy mounds of yellow grain - the treasuries of Pomona and Vertumnus? Such treasuries, in the markets of this world, are worth only a modest so-much-a-bushel, yet I think I should actually feel myself richer with a barrel of apples than with a barrel of money.

From a corn-growing country, we were evidently passing into a country whose beautiful business was apples. Orchards began more or less to line the road, and wagons with those same apple-barrels became a feature of the highway.

Another of its features was the number of old ruined farmhouses we came on, standing side by side with the new, more ambitious homesteads. We seldom came on a prosperous-looking house but a few yards away was to be seen its aged and abandoned parent, smothered up with bushes, roof fallen in, timbers ready to collapse, the deserted hearth choked with debris and overgrown with weeds - the very picture of a haunted house. Here had been the original home, always small, seldom more than four rooms, and when things had begun to prosper, a more spacious, and often, to our eyes, a less attractive, structure had been built, and the old home left to the bats and owls, with a complete abandonment that seemed to us - sentimental travellers as we were - as cynical as it was curiously wasteful.

Putting sentiment out of the question, we had to leave unexplained why the American farmer should thus allow so much good building material to go to waste. Besides, as we also noted much farm machinery rusting unhoused in the grass, we wondered why he did not make use of these old buildings for storage purposes. But the American farmer has puzzled wiser heads than ours, so we gave it up and turned our attention once more to our own fanciful business, one highly useful branch of which was the observation of the names on the tin letter-boxes thrusting themselves out at intervals along the road.

The history of American settlement could, I suppose, be read in those wayside letter-boxes, in such names, for instance, as "Theo. Leveque" and "Paul Fugle," which, like wind-blown exotics from other lands, we found within a few yards of each other. One name, that cf "Silvernail," we decided could only lawfully belong to a princess in a fairy tale. Such childishness as this, I may say, is of the essence of a walking trip, in which, from moment to moment, you take quite infantile interest in all manner of idle observation and quite useless lore. That is a part of the game you are playing, and the main thing is that you are out in the open air, on the open road, with a simple heart and a romantic appetite.

Here is a little picture of a wayfaring day which I made while Colin was sketching one of those ruined farms:

Apples along the highway strewn,
And morning opening all her doors;
The cawing rook, the distant train,
The valley with its misty floors;

The hillside hung with woods and dreams,
Soft gleams of gossamer and dew;
From cockcrow to the rising moon
The rainbowed road for me and you.

Along the highroad all the day
The wagons filled with apples go,
And golden pumpkins and ripe corn,
And all the ruddy overflow

From Autumn's apron, as she goes
About her orchards and her fields,
And gathers into stack and barn
The treasure that the Summer yield.

A singing heart, a laughing road,
With salutations all the way, -
The gossip dog, the hidden bird,
The pig that grunts a gruff good-day;

The apple-ladder in the trees,
A friendly voice amid the boughs,
The farmer driving home his team,
The ducks, the geese, the uddered cows;

The silver babble of the creek,
The willow-whisper - the day's end,
With murmur of the village street,
A called good-night, an unseen friend.

CHAPTER XII

ORCHARDS AND A LINE FROM VIRGIL

Orchards! We were walking to New York - through orchards. And we might have gone by train! A country of orchards and gold-dust sunshine falling through the quaint tapestry trees, falling dreamily on heaped-up gold, and the grave backs of little pigs joyously at large in the apple twilight. A drowsy, murmuring spell was on the land, the spell of fabled orchards, and of old enchanted gardens -

In the afternoon they came unto a land
In which it seemed always afternoon -

the country of King Alcinous. At intervals, as we walked on through the cider-dreamy afternoon, thinking apples, smelling apples, munching apples, there came a mellow sound like soft thunder through the trees. It was the thunder of apples being poured into barrels, and, as in a sleep, the fragrant wagons passed and repassed along the road - "the slow-moving wagons of our lady of Eleusis."

That line of Virgil came to me, as lines will sometimes come in fortunate moments, with the satisfaction of perfect fitness to the hour and the mood, gathering into one sacred, tear-filled phrase the deep sense that had been possessing me, as we passed the husbandmen busy with the various harvest, of the long antiquity of these haunted industries of the earth.

So long, so long, has man pursued these ancient tasks; so long

RICHARD LE GALLIENNE

ago was he urging the plowshare through the furrow, so long ago the sower went forth to sow; so long ago have there been barns and byres, granaries and threshing-floors, mills and vineyards; so long has there been milking of cows, and herding of sheep and swine. Can one see a field of wheat gathered into sheaves without thinking of the dream of Joseph, or be around a farm at lambing time without smiling to recall the cunning of Jacob? Already were all these things weary and old and romantic when Virgil wrote and admo-nished the husbandman of times and seasons, of plows and harrows, of mattocks and hurdles, and the mystical winnowing fan of Iacchus.

To the meditative, romantic mind, the farmer and plowman, standing thus in the foreground of the infinite perspective of time, take on a sacred significance, as of traditional ministers of the ancient mysteries of the earth.

Perhaps it is one's involuntary sense of this haunted antiquity that gives its peculiar expressiveness to the solemn, almost religious quiet of barns and stables, the, so to say, prehistoric hush of brooding, sun-steeped rickyards; and gives, too, a homely, sacerdotal look to the implements and vessels of the farm. A churn or a cheese-press gives one the same deep, uncanny thrill of the terrible vista of time as Stonehenge itself; and from such implements, too, there seems to breathe a sigh - a sigh of the long travail and unbearable pathos of the race of men.

You will thus see the satisfaction, in moods of such meditation, of carrying in one's knapsack a line from Virgil - "the slow-moving wagons of our Lady of Eleusis" - and I congratulated myself on my forethought in having included in our itinerant library a copy of Mr. Mackail's beautiful translation of "The Georgics." Walt Whitman, talking to one of his friends about his habit of carrying a book with him on his nature rambles, said that nine times out of ten he would never open the book, but that the tenth time he would need it very badly. So I needed "The Georgics" very badly that afternoon, and the hour would have lost much of its perfection had I not been able to take the book from my knapsack, and corroborate my mood, while Colin was sketching an old barn, by reading aloud from its consecrated pages:

"I can repeat to thee many a counsel of them of old, if thou shrink not back nor weary to learn of lowly cares. Above all must the threshing-floor be levelled with the ponderous roller, and wrought by hand and cemented with clinging potter's clay, that it may not gather weeds nor crack in the reign of dust, and be playground withal for manifold destroyers. Often the tiny mouse builds his house and makes his granaries underground, or the eyeless mole scoops his cell; and in chinks is found the toad, and all the swarming vermin that are bred in earth; and the weevil, and the ant that fears a destitute old age, plunder the great pile of spelt."

Perhaps some reader had been disposed hastily to say: "What did you want with hooks out of doors? Was not Nature enough?" No one who loves both books and Nature would ask that question, or need to have explained why a knapsack library is a necessary adjunct of a walking-tour.

For Nature and books react so intimately on each other, and, far more than one realizes without thought, our enjoyment of Nature is a creation of literature. For example, can any one sensitive to such considerations deny that the meadows of the world are greener for the Twenty-third Psalm, or the starry sky the gainer in our imagination by the solemn cadences of the book of Job? All our experiences, new and personal as they may seem to us, owe incalculably their depth and thrill to the ancestral sentiment in our blood, and joy and sorrow are for us what they are, no little because so many old, far-away generations of men and women have joyed and sorrowed in the same way before us. Literature but represents that concentrated sentiment, and satisfies through expression our human need for some sympathetic participation with us in our human experience.

That a long-dead poet walking in the Spring was moved as I

am by the unfolding leaf and the returning bird imparts an added significance to my own feelings; and that some wise and beautiful old book knew and said it all long ago, makes my life seem all the more mysteriously romantic for me to-day. Besides, books are not only such good companions for what they say, but for what they are. As with any other friend, you may go a whole day with them, and not have a word to say to each other, yet be happily conscious of a perfect companionship. The book we know and love - and, of course, one would never risk taking a book we didn't know for a companion - has long since become a symbol for us, a symbol of certain moods and ways of feeling, a key to certain kingdoms of the spirit, of which it is often sufficient just to hold the key in our hands. So, a single flower in the hand is a key to Summer, a floating perfume the key to the hidden gardens of remembrance. The wrong book in the hand, whether opened or not, is as distracting a presence as an irrelevant person; and therefore it was with great care that I chose my knapsack library. It consisted of these nine books:

Mackail's "Georgics."
Hans Andersen's Fairy Tales.
Shakespeare's Sonnets.
Locke's "Beloved Vagabond."
Selections from R.L.S
Pater's "Marius the Epicurean."
Alfred de Musset's "Premieres Poesies."
Baedeker's "United States."
Road Map of New York State.

And, though my knapsack already weighed eighteen pounds, I could not resist the call of a cheap edition of Wordsworth in a drug-store at Warsaw, a charming little town embosomed among hills and orchards, where we arrived, dreamy with country air, at the end of the day.

CHAPTER XIII

FELLOW WAYFARERS

With the morn our way still lay among apples and honey, hives and orchards; a land of prosperous farms, sumptuous rolling downs, rich woodland, sheep, more pigs, more apple-barrels and velvety sunshine. The old ruined houses had ceased, and the country had taken on a more generous, broad-shouldered, deep-bosomed aspect. Nature was preparing for one of her big Promised Land effects. We were coming to the valley of the Genesee River. We made a comparison of two kinds of prosperity in the look of a landscape. Some villages and farms suggest smugness in their prosperity. They have a model-farm, business-like, well-regulated, up-to-date, company-financed air, suggesting such modern agricultural terms as "ensilage," "irrigation" and "fertilizer." Other villages and farms, while just as well-kept and well-to-do, have, so to say, a something romantic about their prosperity, a bounteous, ruddy, golden-age look about them, as though Nature herself had been the farmer and they had ruddied and ripened out of her own unconscious abundance - the difference between a row of modern box beehives and the old thatched-cottage kind. The countryside of the Genesee valley has the romantic prosperous look. Its farms and villages look like farms and villages in picture-books, and the country folk we met seemed happy and gay and kind, such as those one reads of in William Morris's romances of the golden age. As from time to time we exchanged greetings with them, we were struck with their comely health and blithe ways - particularly with their fine teeth, as they laughed us the time of day, or stopped their

RICHARD LE GALLIENNE

wagons to gossip a moment with the two outlandish packmen - the very teeth one would expect in an apple-country. Perhaps they came of so much sweet commerce with apples!

The possessor of a particularly fine display hailed us as he drove by in an empty wagon, at the tail of which trailed a long orchard ladder, and asked us if we would care for a lift. Now it happened that his suggestion came like a voice from heaven for poor Colin, one of whose shoes had been casting a gloom over our spirits for several miles. So we accepted with alacrity, and, really, riding felt quite good for a change! Our benefactor was a bronzed, handsome young fellow, just through Cornell, he told us, and proud of his brave college, as all Cornell men are. He had chosen apple-farming for his career, and, naturally, seemed quite happy about it; lived on his farm near by with his mother and sister, and was at the moment out on the quest of four apple-packers for his harvesting, these experts being at a premium at this season. We rattled along gaily in the broad afternoon sunshine, exchanging various human information, from apple-packing to New York theatres, after the manner of the companionable soul of man, and I hope he liked us as well as we liked him.

One piece of information was of particular interest to Colin, the whereabouts of one "Billy the Cobbler," a character of the neighbourhood, who would fix Colin's shoe for him, and, incidentally, if he was in the mood, give us a musical and dramatic entertainment into the bargain.

At length our ways parted, and, with cheery good-byes and good wishes, our young friend went rattling along, leaving in our hearts a warm feeling of the brotherhood of man - sometimes. He had let us down close by the "High Banks," the rumour of which had been in our ears for some miles, and presently the great effect Nature had been preparing burst on our gaze with a startling surprise. The peaceful pastoral country was suddenly cloven in twain by a gigantic chasm, the Genesee River, dizzy depths below, picturesquely flowing between Grand Canon rock effects, shaggy woods clothing the precipitous limestone, and small forests growing far down in the broad bed of the river, with here and there checker-board spaces of cultivated land, gleaming, smooth and green, amid all the spectacular savageness - soft, cozy spots of verdure nestling dreamily in the hollow of the giant rocky hand. The road ran close to the edge of the chasm, and the sublimity was with us, laying its hush upon us, for the rest of the afternoon. Appropriate to her Jove-like mood, Nature had planted stern thickets of oak-trees along the rocky edge, and "the acorns of our lord of Chaonia" crunched beneath our feet as we walked on.

After a while, sure enough we came upon "Billy the Cobbler," seated at his bench in a little shop at the beginning of a straggle of houses, alone, save for his cat, at the sleepy end of afternoon. We had understood that he had been crippled in some cruel accident of machinery, and was hampered in the use of his legs. But, unless in a certain philosophic sweetness on his big, happy face, there was no sign of the cripple about his burly, broad-shouldered personality. He was evidently meant to be a giant, and was what one might call the bo'sun type, bluff, big-voiced and merry, with a boyish laugh, large, twinkling eyes, a trifle wistful, and the fine teeth of the district.

"Well, boys," said he, looking up from his work with a smile, "and what can I do for you? Walking, eh? - to New York!" and he whistled, as every one did when they learned our mysterious business.

Then, taking Colin's shoe in his hand, he commenced to pound upon that instrument of torture, talking gaily the while. Presently he asked, "Do you care about music?" and on our eagerly agreeing that we did, "All right," he said, "we'll close the shop for a few minutes and have some."

Then, moving around on his seat, like some heroic half-figure bust on its pedestal, he rummaged among the litter of leather and tools at his side, and produced a guitar from its baize bag, also a mouth organ, which by some ingenious wire arrangement he fastened around his neck, so that he might press his lips upon it, leaving his hands free for the guitar.

Then, "Ready?" said he, and, applying himself simultaneously to the guitar and the harmonica, off he started with a quite electrical gusto into a spirited fandango that made the little shop dance and rattle with merriment. You would have said that a whole orchestra was there, such a volume and variety of musical sound did Billy contrive to evoke from his two instruments.

"There!" he said, with a humorous chuckle, pushing the harmonica aside from his mouth, "what do you think of that for an overture?" He had completely hypnotized us with his infectious high spirits, and we were able to applaud him sincerely, for this lonely cobbler of shoes was evidently a natural well of music, and was, besides, no little of an executant.

"Now I'll give you an imitation of grand opera," he said; and then he launched into the drollest burlesque of a fashionable tenor and a prima-donna, as clever as could be. He was evidently a born mime as well as a musician, and presently delighted us with some farmyard imitations, and one particularly quaint impersonation, "an old lady singing with false teeth," sent us into fits of laughter.

"You ought to go into vaudeville," we both said spontaneously, with that vicious modern instinct to put private gifts to professional uses, and then Billy, with shy pride, admitted that he did do a little now and again in a professional way at harvest balls (we thought of Sheldon Center) and the like.

"Perhaps you might like one of my professional letter-heads," he said, handing us one apiece. I think probably the reader would like one, too. You must imagine it in the original, with fancy displayed professional type, regular "artiste" style, and a portrait of Billy, with his two instruments, in one corner. And "see thou mock him not," gentle reader!

King of Them All
BILLY WILLIAMS
THE KING OF ALL IMITATORS
Producing in Rapid Succession
A GRAND REPERTOIRE
of Imitations and Impersonations
Consisting of:

Minstrel Bands, Circus Bands, Killing
Pigs, Cat Greeting Her Kitten, Barn-Yard
of Hens and Roosters, Opera
Singers with Guitar, Whistling with
Guitar, Old Lady Singing with False
Teeth, Cow and Calf, Harmonica with
the Guitar, Arab Song, Trombone Solo
with the Guitar.

Yes! "See thou mock him not," gentle reader, for Billy is no subject for any man's condescension. We were in his company scarcely an hour, but we went away with a great feeling of respect and tenderness for him, and we hope some day to drop in on him again, and hear his music and his quaint, manly wisdom.

"All alone in the world, Billy?"

A shade of sadness passed over his face, and was gone again, as he smilingly answered, stroking the cat that purred and rubbed herself against his shoulder.

"Just puss and me and the guitar," he said. "The happiest of families. Ah! Music's a great thing of a lonely evening."

And a sense of the brave loneliness of Billy's days swept over me as we shook his strong hand, and he gave us a cheery godspeed on our way. I am convinced that Billy could earn quite a salary on the vaudeville stage; but - no! he is better where he is, sitting there at his bench, with his black cat and his guitar and his singing, manly soul.

The twilight was rapidly thickening as we left Billy, once more bent over his work, and, the fear of "supper-time" in our hearts, we pushed on at extra speed toward our night's lodging at Mount Morris. The oak-trees gloomed denser on our right as we plowed along a villainously sandy road. Labourers homing from the day's work greeted us now and again in the dimness, and presently one of these, plodding up behind us, broke forth into conversation:

"Ben-a carry pack-a lik-a dat-a - forty-two months - army - ol-a country," said the voice out of the darkness.

It was an Italian labourer on his way to supper, interested in our knapsacks.

"You're an Italian?"

"Me come from Pal-aer-mo."

The little chap was evidently in a talkative mood, and I nudged Colin to do the honours of the conversation.

"Pal-aer-mo? Indeed!" said Colin. "Fine city, I guess."

"Been-a Pal-aer-mo?" asked the Italian eagerly. Colin couldn't say that he had.

"Great city, Pal-aer-mo," continued our friend, "great theatre - cost sixteen million dollars."

There is nothing like a walking-trip for gathering information of this kind.

The Italian went on to explain that this country was a poor substitute for the "ol-a country."

"This country - rough country. In this country me do rough-a work," he explained apologetically; "in Pal-aer-mo do polit-a work."

And he accentuated his statement by a vicious side spit upon the American soil.

It transpired that the "polit-a work" on which he had been engaged in Pal-aer-mo had been waiting in a restaurant.

And so the poor soul chattered on, touching, not unintelligently, in his absurd English, on American politics, capital and labour, the rich and the poor. The hard lot of the poor man in America, and - "Pal-aer-mo," made the recurring burden of his talk, through which, a pathetic undertone, came to us a sense of the native poetry of his race.

Did he ever expect to return to Palermo? we asked him as we parted. "Ah! many a night me dream of Pal-aer-mo," he called back, as, striking into a by-path, he disappeared in the darkness.

And then we came to a great iron bridge, sternly silhouetted in the sunset. On either side rose cliffs of darkness, and beneath, like sheets of cold moonlight, flowed the Genesee, a Dantesque effect of jet and silver, Stygian in its intensity and indescribably mournful. The banks of Acheron can not be more wildly *funebre*, and it was companionable to hear Colin's voice mimicking out of the darkness:

"In this country me do rough-a work. In Pal-aer-mo do polit-work!"

"Poor chap!" I said, after a pause, thinking of our friend from Pal-aer-mo. "Do you know Hafiz, Colin?" I continued. "There is an ode of his that came back to me as our poor Italian was talking. I think I will say it to you. It is just the time and place for it."

"Do," said Colin. And then I repeated:

> *"At sunset, when the eyes of exiles fill,*
> *And distance makes a desert of the heart,*

And all the lonely world grows lonelier still,
I with the other exiles go apart,
And offer up the stranger's evening prayer.
My body shakes with weeping as I pray,
Thinking on all I love that are not there,
So desolately absent far away -
My Love and Friend, and my own land and home.
O aching emptiness of evening skies!
O foolish heart, what tempted thee to roam
So far away from the Beloved's eyes!
To the Beloved's country I belong -
I am a stranger in this foreign place;
Strange are its streets, and strange to me its tongue;
Strange to the stranger each familiar face.
'Tis not my city! Take me by the hand,
Divine protector of the lonely ones,
And lead me back to the Beloved's land -
Back to my friends and my companions
O wind that blows from Shiraz, bring to me
A little dust from my Beloved's street;
Send Hafiz something, love, that comes from thee,
Touched by thy hand, or trodden by thy feet."

"My! but that makes one feel lonesome," was Colin's comment. "I wonder if there will be any mail from the folk at Mount Morris."

CHAPTER XIV

THE OLD LADY OF THE WALNUTS AND OTHERS

What manner of men we were and what our business was, thus wandering along the highroads with packs on our backs and stout sticks in our hands, was matter for no little speculation, and even suspicion, to the rural mind. We did not seem to fit in with any familiar classification of vagabond. We might be peddlers, or we might be "hoboes," but there was a disquieting uncertainty about us, and we felt it necessary occasionally to make reassuring explanations. Once or twice we found no opportunity to do this, as, for instance, one sinister, darksome evening, we stood in hesitation at a puzzling cross-road - near Dansville, I think - and awaited the coming of an approaching buggy from which to ask the way. It was driven by two ladies, who, on our making a signal of distress to them, immediately whipped up with evident alarm, and disappeared in a flash. Dear things! they evidently anticipated a hold-up, and no doubt arrived home with a breathless tale of two suspicious-looking characters hanging about the neighbourhood.

On another occasion, we had been seated awhile under a walnut tree growing near a farm, and scattering its fruitage half across the highroad. Colin had been anointing his suffering foot, and, as I told him, looked strongly reminiscent of a certain famous corn-cure advertisement. Meanwhile, I had been once more quoting Virgil: "The walnut in the woodland attires herself in wealth of blossom and bends with scented boughs," when there approached with slow step an old, white-haired lady, at once gentle and severe in appearance, accompanied by a younger lady. When they had arrived in front of us, the old lady in measured tones of sorrow rather than anger, said: "We rather needed those walnuts - " Dear soul! she evidently thought that we had been filling our knapsacks with her nuts, and it took some little astonished expostulation on our part to convince her that we hadn't. This affront seemed to sink no little into Colin's sensitive Latin soul - and they were public enough walnuts, anyway, scattered, as they were, across the public road! But Colin couldn't get over it for some time, and I suspected that he was the more sensitive from his recently - owing, doubtless, to his distinguished Gallic appearance - having been profanely greeted by some irreverent boys with the word "Spaghetti!" However, there was balm for our wounded feelings a little farther along the road, when a companionable old farmer greeted us with:

"Well, boys! out for a walk? It's easy seeing you're no tramps."

Colin's expression was a study in gratitude. The farmer was a fine, soldierly old fellow, who told me that he was half English, too, on his father's side.

"But my mother," he added, "was a good blue-bellied Yankee."

We lured him on to using that delightfully quaint expression again before we left him; and we also learned from him valuable information as to the possibilities of lunch farther along the road, for we were in a lonely district with no inns, and it was Sunday.

In regard to lunch, I suppose that in prosaically paying our way for bed and board as we fared along we fell short of the Arcadian theory of walking-tours in which the wayfarer, like a mendicant friar, takes toll of lunch and dinner from the hospitable farmer of sentimental legend, and sleeps for choice in barns, hayricks or hedgesides. Now, sleeping out of doors in October, if you have ever tried it, is a very different thing from sleeping out of doors in June, and as for rural hospitality - well, if you are of a sensitive constitution you shrink from obtruding yourself, an alien apparition, upon the embarrassed and embarrassing rural domesticities. Besides, to be quite honest, rural table-talk, except in Mr. Hardy's novels or pastoral poetry, is, to say the least, lacking in variety. Indeed, if the truth must be told, the conversation of country people, generally speaking, and an occasional, very occasional, character or oddity apart, is undeniably dull, and I hope it will not be imputed to me for hardness of heart that, after some long-winded colloquy or endless reminiscence, sententious and trivial, I have thought that Gray's famous line should really have been written - "the long and tedious annals of the poor."

But my heart smites me with ingratitude toward some kindly memories as I write that - memories of homely welcome, simple and touching and dignified. Surely I am not writing so of the genial farmer on whom we came one lunch hour as he was stripping corn in his yard.

"Missus," he called to the house a few yards away, "can you find any lunch for two good-looking fellows here?"

The housewife came to the door, scanned us for a second, and replied in the affirmative. As we sat down to table, our host bowed his head and said a simple grace for the bacon and cabbage, pumpkin-pie, cheese and tea we were about to receive; and the unexpected old-fashioned rite, too seldom encountered nowadays, came on me with a fresh beauty and impressiveness, which made me feel that its discontinuance is a real loss of gracious ritual in our lives, and perhaps even more. Thus this simple farmer's board seemed sensitively linked with the far-away beginnings of time. Of all our religious symbolism, the country gods and the gods of the hearth and the household seem actual, approachable presences, and the saying of grace before meat was a beautiful, fitting reminder of that mysterious, invisible care and sustenance of our lives, which no longer find any recognition in our daily routine: *Above all, worship thou the gods, and bring great Ceres her yearly offerings.*

RICHARD LE GALLIENNE

Another such wayside meal and another old couple live touchingly in our memories. We were still in the broad, sun-swept valley of the Genesee, our road lying along the edge of the wide, reed-grown flats and water-meadows, bounded on the north by rolling hills. On our left hand, parallel with the road, ran a sort of willowed moat banked by a grass-grown causeway, a continuous narrow mound, somewhat higher than the surrounding country, and cut through here and there with grass-grown gullies, the whole suggesting primeval earthworks and excavations. So the old Roman roads run, grassy and haunted and choked with underbrush, in the lonelier country districts of England. We were curious as to the meaning of this causeway, and learned at length that here was all that remained of the old Genesee Canal. Thirty years ago, this moat had brimmed with water, and barges had plied their sleepy traffic between Dansville and Rochester. But the old order had changed, and a day had come when the dike had been cut through, the lazy water let out into the surrounding flats, and the old waterway left to the willows and the wild-flowers, the mink and the musk-rat. Only thirty years ago - yet to-day Nature has so completely taken it all back to herself that the hush of a long-vanished antiquity is upon it, and the turfy burial mound of some Hengist and Horsa could not be more silent.

This old fosse seemed to strike the somewhat forgotten, out-of-the-world note of the surrounding country. Picturesque to the eye, with bounteous green prospects and smooth, smiling hills, it was not, we were told, as prosperous as it looked. For some vague reason, the tides of agricultural prosperity had ebbed from that spacious sunlit vale. A handsome old trapper, who sat at his house door smoking his pipe and looking across the green flats, set down the cause to the passing of the canal. Ah, yes! it was possible for him, thirty years ago, to make the trip to Rochester and back by the canal, and bring home a good ten dollars; but now - well, every one in the valley was poor, except the man whose beehives we had seen on the hillside half-a-mile back. He had made no less than a thousand dollars out of his honey this last season. He was an old bachelor, too, like himself. There were no less than five bachelors in the valley - five old men without a woman to look after them.

"- or bother them," the old chap added humorously, relighting his pipe. Mrs. Mulligan, half a mile farther up the valley, was the only woman thereabouts; and she, by the way, would give us some lunch. We could say that he had sent us.

So we left the old trapper to his pipe and his memories, and went in search of Mrs. Mulligan. Presently a poor little house high up on the hillside caught our eye, and we made toward it. As we were nearing the door, a dog, evidently not liking our packs, sprang out at us, and from down below in the marshy flats floated the voice of a man calling to us.

"Get out o' that!" hailed the voice. "There's nothing there for you."

Poor Colin! We were evidently taken for tramps once more.

However, undaunted by this reception, we reached the cottage door, and at our knock appeared a very old, but evidently vigorous, woman.

"Is this Mrs. Mulligan's house?"

Her name on the lips of two strangers brought a surprised smile to her face - a pleasant feeling of importance, even notoriety, no doubt - and she speedily made us welcome, and, with many apologies, set before us the cold remains of lunch which had been over an hour or two ago - cold squash, pumpkin pie, cheese and milk. It was too bad we were late, for they had had a chicken for dinner, and had sent the remains of it to a friend down the road, - our trapper, no doubt, - and if the fire hadn't gone out she would have made us some tea. Now, cold squash is not exactly an inflammatory diet, but we liked the old lady so much, she had such a pleasant, motherly way with her, and such an entertaining, wise and even witty tongue, that we decided that cold squash, with her as hostess, was better than a stalled ox and hatred therewith.

Presently the door opened and the good man entered, he who had called to us from the marsh - a tall, emaciated old man, piteously thin, and old, and work-weary to look on, but with a keen, bright eye in his head, and something of a proud air about his ancient figure. It seemed cruel to think of his old bones having still to go on working, but our two old people, who seemed pathetically fond of each other, were evidently very poor, like the rest of the valley. The old man excused himself for his salutation of us - but there were so many dangerous characters about, and the old folk shook their heads and told of the daring operations of mysterious robbers in the neighbourhood. In their estimation, the times were generally unsafe, and lawless characters rife in the land. We looked around at the pathetic poverty of the place - and wondered why they should disquiet themselves. Poor souls! there was little left to rob them of, save the fluttering remnants of their mortal breath. But, poor as they were, they had their telephone, - a fact that struck us paradoxically in many a poor cabin as we went along. Yes! had they a mind, they could call up the White House, that instant, or the Waldorf-Astoria.

We spoke of our old trapper, and the old lady smiled.

"Those are his socks I've been darning for him," she said. So the cynical old bachelor was taken care of by the good angel, woman, after all!

Trapping was about all there was to do now in the valley, she said. A mink brought seven dollars, a musk-rat thirty cents. Our old bachelor had made as much as eighteen dollars in two days - one day several years ago. The old man had told us this himself. It was evidently quite a piece of history in the valley, quite a local legend.

CHAPTER XV

THE MAN AT DANSVILLE

At Dansville we fell in with a man after our own hearts. Fortunately for himself and his friends, he is unaware of the simple fact that he is a poet. We didn't tell him, either - though we longed to. He was standing outside his prosperous-looking planing-mill, at about half-past eight of a dreaming October morning. Inside, the saws were making that droning, sweet-smelling, sawdust noise that made Colin think of "Adam Bede." The willows and button-wood trees at the back of the workshops were still smoking with sunlit mist, and the quiet, massive, pretty water looked like a sleepy mirror, as it softly flooded along to its work on the big, dripping wheels.

To our left a great hill, all huge and damp, glittering with gossamers, and smelling of restless yellow leaves, shouldered the morning sky.

Then, turning away from talk with three or four workmen, standing at his office door, he saluted the two apparitional figures, so oddly passing along the muddy morning road.

"Out for a walk, boys?" he called.

He was a handsome man of about forty-three, with a romantic scar slashed down his left cheek, a startling scar that must have meant hideous agony to him, and yet, here in the end, had made his face beautiful, by the presence in it of a spiritual conquest.

RICHARD LE GALLIENNE

"How far are you walking? - you are not going so far as my little river here, I'll bet -"

And then we understood that we were in the presence of romantic conversation, and we listened with a great gladness.

"Yes! who would think that this little, quiet, mill-race is on her way to the Gulf of Mexico!"

We looked at the little reeded river, so demure in her morning mists, so discreet and hushed among her willows, and in our friend's eyes, and by the magic of his fanciful tongue, we saw her tripping along to dangerous conjunctions with resounding rock-bedded streams, adventurously taking hands with swirling, impulsive floods, fragrant with water-flowers and laden with old forests, and at length, through the strange, starlit hills, sweeping out into some moonlit estuary of the all-enfolding sea.

"Aren't you glad we walked, Colin?" I said, a mile or two after. "You are, of course, a great artist; but I don't remember you ever having a thought quite so fine and romantic as that, do you?"

"How strange it must be," said Colin, after a while, "to have beauty - beautiful thoughts, beautiful pictures - merely as a recreation; not as one's business, I mean. And the world is full of people who have no need to sell their beautiful thoughts!"

CHAPTER XVI

IN WHICH WE CATCH UP WITH SUMMER

Some eminent wayfarers - one peculiarly beloved - have discoursed on the romantic charm of maps. But they have dwelt chiefly on the suggestiveness of them before the journey: these unknown names of unknown places, in types of mysteriously graduated importance - what do they stand for? These mazy lines, some faint and wayward as a hair, and some straight and decided as a steel track - whence and whither do they lead? I love the map best when the journey is done - when I can pore on its lines as into the lined face of some dear friend with whom I have travelled the years, and say - here this happened, here that befell! This almost invisible dot is made of magic rocks and is filled with the song of rapids; this infinitesimal fraction of "Scale five miles to the inch" is a haunted valley of purple pine-woods, and the moon rising, and the lonely cry of a sheep that has lost her little one somewhere in the folds of the hills. Here, where is no name, stands an old white church with a gilded cross, among little white houses huddled together under a bluff. In yonder garden the priest's cassock and trousers are hanging sacrilegiously on a clothes-line, and you can just see a tiny graveyard away up on the hillside almost hidden in the trees.

Even sacred vestments must be laundered by earthly laundresses, yet somehow it gives one a shock to see sacred vestments out of the sanctuary, profanely displayed on a clothes-line. It is as though one should turn the sacred chalice into a tea-pot. A priest's trousers on a clothes-line might well be the beginning of atheism. But I hope there were no such fanciful deductive minds in that peaceful hamlet, and that the faithful there can withstand even so profound a trial of faith. If it had been my own creed that those vestments represented, I should have been shaken, I confess; and, as it was, I felt a vague pain of disillusionment, of an indignity done to the unseen; as, whatever the creed, living or dead, may be, I always feel in those rooms often affected by artistic people, furnished with the bric-a-brac of religions, indeed not their own, but, none the less, once or even now, the living religions of other people - rooms in which forgotten, or merely foreign, deities are despitefully used for decoration, and a crucifix and a Buddha and an African idol alike parts of the artistic furniture. But, no doubt, it is to consider too curiously to consider so, and the good priest whose cassock and trousers have occasioned these reflections would smilingly prick my fancies, after the dialectic manner of his calling, and say that his trousers on the clothes-line were but a humble reminder to the faithful how near to the daily life of her children, how human at once as well as divine, is Mother Church.

A cross, naturally, marks the spot where we saw those priest's trousers on the line; but there are no crosses for a hundred places of memorable moments of our journey; they must go without memorial even in this humble record, and Colin and I must be content to keep wayside shrines for them in our hearts.

How insignificant, on the map, looks the little stretch of some seventeen miles from Dansville to Cohocton, yet I feel that one would need to erect a cathedral to represent the perfect day of golden October wayfaring it stands for, as on the weather-beaten map spread out before me on my writing-table, as Colin and I so often spread it out under a tree by some lonely roadside, I con the place-names that to us "bring a perfume in the mention." It was a district of quaint, romantic-sounding names, and it fully justified that fantastic method of choosing our route by the sound of the names of places, which I confessed to the reader on an earlier page: Wayland - Patchin's

Mills - Blood's Depot - Cohocton. And to north and south of our route were names such as Ossian, Stony Brook Glen, Loon Lake, Rough & Ready, Doly's Corners, and Neil Creek. I confess that there was a Perkinsville to go through - a beautiful spot, too, for which one felt that sort of aesthetic pity one feels for a beautiful girl married to a man, say, of the name of Podgers. Perkinsville! It was as though you said - the beautiful Mrs. Podgers. But there was consolation in the sound of Wayland, with its far call to Wayland's smithy and Walter Scott. And - Cohocton! The name to me had a fine Cromwellian ring; and Blood's Depot - what a truculent sound to that! - if you haven't forgotten the plumed dare-devil cavalier who once made a dash to steal the king's regalia from the Tower. Again - Loon Lake. Can you imagine two more lonesome wailing words to make a picture with? But - Cohocton. How oddly right my absurd instinct had been about that - and, shall we ever forget the unearthly beauty of the evening which brought us at dark to the quaint little operatic-looking village, deep and snug among the solemn, sleeping hills?

The day had been one of those days that come perhaps only in October - days of rich, languorous sunshine full of a mysterious contentment, days when the heart says, "My cup runneth over," and happy tears suddenly well to the eyes, as though from a deep overflowing sense of the goodness of God. It was really Summer, with the fragrant mists of Autumn in her hair. It had happened as we had hoped on starting out. We had caught up with Summer on her way to New York, Summer all her golden self, though garlanded with wreaths of Autumn, and about her the swinging censers of burning weeds.

It was a wonderful valley we had caught her in, all rolling purple hills softly folding and unfolding in one continuous causeway; a narrow valley, and the hills were high and close and gentle, suggesting protection and abundance and never-ending peace. Here and there the vivid green of Winter wheat struck a note of Spring amid all the mauves and ochres of dying things.

RICHARD LE GALLIENNE

It was a day on which you had no wish to talk, - you were too happy, - wanted only to wander on and on as in a dream through the mellow vale - one of those days in which the world seems too good to be true, a day of which we feel, "This day can never come again." It was like walking through the Twenty-third Psalm. And, as it closed about us, as we came to our village at nightfall, and the sunshine, like a sinking lake of gold, grew softer and softer behind the uplands, the solid world of rock and tree, and stubble-field and clustered barns, seemed to be growing pure thought - nothing seemed left of it but spirit; and the hills had become as the luminous veil of some ineffable temple of the mysterious dream of the world.

"Puvis de Chavannes!" said Colin to me in a whisper.

And later I tried to say better what I meant in this song:

Strange, at this still enchanted hour,
How things in daylight hard and rough,
Iron and stone and cruel power,
Turn to such airy, starlit stuff!

Yon mountain, vast as Behemoth,
Seems but a veil of silver breath;
And soundless as a flittering moth,
And gentle as the face of death,

Stands this stern world of rock and tree
Lost in some hushed sidereal dream -
The only living thing a bird,
The only moving thing a stream.

And, strange to think, yon silent star,
So soft and safe amid the spheres -
Could we but see and hear so far -
Is made of thunder, too, and tears.

CHAPTER XVII

CONTAINING VALUABLE STATISTICS

And the morning was like unto the evening. Summer was still to be our companion, and, as the evening of our coming to Cohocton had been the most dreamlike of all the ends of our walking days - had, so to say, been most evening-spiritual, so the morning of our Cohocton seemed most morning-spiritual of all our mornings, most filled with strange hope and thrill and glitter. We were afoot earlier than usual. The sun had hardly risen, and the shining mists still wreathed the great hill which overhangs the village. We were for calling it a mountain, but we were told that it lacked fifty feet of being a mountain. You are not a mountain till you grow to a thousand feet. Our mountain was only some nine hundred and fifty feet. Therefore, it was only entitled to be called a hill. I love information - don't you, dear reader? - though, to us humble walking delegates of the ideal, it was all one. But I know for certain that it was a lane of young maples which made our avenue of light-hearted departure out of the village, though I cannot be sure of the names of all the trees of the thick woods which clothed the hillside beneath which our road lay, a huge endless hillside all dripping and sparkling, and alive with little rills, facing a broad plain, a sea of feathery grass almost unbearably beautiful with soft glittering dew and opal mists, out of which rose spectral elms, like the shadows of gigantic Shanghai roosters. All about was the sound of brooks musically rippling from the hills, and there was a chaste chill in the air, as befitted the time of day, for

Maiden still the morn is, and strange she is, and secret,
Her cheeks are cold as cold sea-shells.

It was all so beautiful that an old thought came back to me
that I often had as a child, when I used to be taken among
mysterious mountains, for Summer holidays: Do people really
live in such beautiful places all the year round? Do they live
there just like ordinary people in towns, go about ordinary
businesses, live ordinary lives? It seemed to me then, as it seems
to me still, that such places should be kept sacred, like
fairyland, or should, at least, be the background of high and
romantic action, like the scenery in operas. To think of a valley
so beautiful as that through which we were walking being put
to any other use than that of beauty seems preposterous; but
do you know what that beautiful valley was doing, while Colin
and I were thus poetizing it, adoring its outlines and revelling
in its tints? It was just quietly growing potatoes. Yes! we had
mostly passed through the apple country. This garden of Eden,
this Vale of Enna, was a great potato country. And we learned,
too, that its inhabitants were by no means so pleased with
beautiful Cohoctori Valley as we were. Here, we gathered, was
another beautiful ne'er-do-well of Nature, too occupied with
her good looks to be fit for much else than prinking herself out
with wild-flowers, and falling into graceful attitudes before her
mirror - and there were mirrors in plenty, many streams and
willows, in Cohocton Valley; everywhere, for us, the
mysterious charm of running water. Once this idle daughter of
Ceres used to grow wheat, wheat "in great plenty," but now
she could be persuaded to grow nothing but potatoes.

All this and much more we learned from a friend who drew up
beside us in a buggy, as I was drinking from a gleaming thread
of water gliding down a mossed conduit of hollowed tree-
trunks into an old cauldron sunk into the hillside, and long
since turned in ferns and lichen. Colin was seated near by
making a sketch, as I drank.

"I wouldn't drink too much of that water, lads," said the
friendly voice of the dapper little intelligent-faced man in

the buggy.

What! not drink this fairy water?

"Why, you country folk are as afraid of fresh water as you are of fresh air," I answered, laughing.

"All right, it's up to you - but it's been a dry Summer, you know."

And then the little man's attention was taken by Colin.

"Sketching?" he asked, and then he said, half shyly, "Would you mind my taking a look how you do it?" and, climbing down from his buggy, he came and looked over Colin's shoulder. "I used to try my hand at it a bit when I was a boy, but those blamed trees always beat me ... don't bother you much, seemingly though," he added, as he watched Colin's pencil with the curiosity of a child.

"I've a little girl at home who does pretty well," he continued after a moment, "but you've certainly got her skinned. I wish she could see you doing it."

His delight in a form of skill which has always been as magical to me as it seemed to him, was charmingly boyish, and Colin turned over his sketch-book, and showed him the notes he had made as we went along. One of a stump fence particularly delighted him - those stump fences made out of the roots of pine trees set side by side, which had been a feature of the country some miles back, and which make such a weird impression on the landscape, like rows of gigantic black antlers, or many-armed Hindoo idols, or a horde of Zulus in fantastic war-gear drawn up in battle-array, or the blackened stumps of giants' teeth - Colin and I tried all those images and many more to express the curious weird effect of coming upon them in the midst of a green and smiling landscape.

"Well, lads," he said, after we had talked awhile, "I shall have to be going. But you've given me a great deal of pleasure. Can't I give you a lift in exchange? I guess there is room for the three of us."

Now Colin and I, on the occasion of our ride with the apple-farmer, awhile back, had held subtle casuistical debate on the legitimacy of men ostensibly, not to say ostentatiously, on foot to New York picking up chance rides in this way. The argument had gone into pursuit of very fine distinctions, and almost rivalled in its casuistry the famous old Duns Scotus - or was it Thomas Aquinas? - debate as to how many angels can dance on the point of a needle. Once we had come to a deadlock as to the kind of vehicle from which it was proper to accept such hospitality. Perhaps it was a Puritan scrupulousness in my blood that had made me take the stand that four-wheeled vehicles, such as wagons, hay-carts and the like, being slow-moving, were permissible, but that buggies, or any form of rapid two-wheeled vehicle, were not. To this Colin had retorted that, on that basis, a tally-ho would be all right, or even an automobile. So the argument had wrestled from side to side, and finally we had compromised.

We agreed that an occasional buggy would be within the vagabond law and that any vehicle, other, of course, than an automobile, which was not plying for hire - such as a trolley or a local train - might on occasion be gratefully climbed into.

Thus it was that we hesitated a moment at the offer of our friend, a hesitancy we amused him by explaining as, presently, conscience-clear, we rattled with him through the hills. He was an interesting talker, a human-hearted, keen-minded man, and he had many more topics as well as potatoes. Besides, he was not in the potato business, but, as with our former friend, his beautiful business was apples. Still, he talked very entertainingly about potatoes; telling us, among other things, that, so friendly was the soil toward that particular vegetable that it yielded as much as a hundred to a hundred and fifty bushels to the acre, and that a fair-sized potato farm thereabouts, properly handled, would pay for itself in a year. I transcribe this information, not merely because I think that, among so many words, the reader is fairly entitled to expect some little information, but chiefly for the benefit of a friend of mine, the like of whom, no doubt, the reader counts among his acquaintances. The friend I mean has a mind so quaintly voracious of facts that, often when we have been dining together at one of the great hotels, he would speculate, say, looking round the room filled with eager diners, on how many clams are nightly consumed in New York City, or how many millions of fresh eggs New York requires each morning for breakfast. So when next I dine with him I will say, as he asks me about my trip:

"Do you know that in the Cohocton Valley they raise as much as one hundred to one hundred and fifty bushels of potatoes to the acre?" And he will say:

"You don't really mean to say so?"

I have in my private note-book much more such tabulated information which I picked up and hoarded for his entertainment, just as whenever a letter comes to me from abroad, I tear off the stamp and save it for a little girl I love.

But, as I said, our friend in the buggy was by no means limited to potatoes for his conversation. He was learned in the geography of the valley and told us how once the Cohocton River, now merely a decorative stream among willows, was once a serviceable waterway, how it was once busy with mills, and how men used to raft down it as far as Elmira.

But "the springs were drying up." I liked the mysterious sound of that, and still more his mysterious story of an undercurrent from the Great Lakes that runs beneath the valley. I seemed to hear the sound of its strange subterranean flow as he talked. Such is the fun of knowing so little about the world. The simplest fact out of a child's geography thus comes to one new and marvellous.

Well, we had to say good-bye at last to our friend at a cross-road, and we left him learnedly discussing the current prices of apples with a business acquaintance who had just driven up - Kings, Rambos, Baldwins, Greenings, and Spigs. And, by the way, in packing apples into barrels, you must always pack them - stems down. Be careful to remember that.

CHAPTER XVIII

A DITHYRAMBUS OF BUTTEEMILK

One discovery of some importance you make in walking the roads is the comparative rarity and exceeding preciousness of buttermilk. We had, as I said, caught up with Summer. Summer, need one say, is a thirsty companion, and the State seemed suddenly to have gone dry. We looked in vain for magic mirrors by the roadside, overhung with fairy grasses, littered with Autumn leaves, and skated over by nimble water-bugs. As our friend had said, the springs seemed to have dried up. Now and again we would hail with a great cry a friendly pump; once we came upon a cider-mill, but it was not working, and time and again we knocked and asked in vain for buttermilk. Sometimes, but not often, we found it. Once we met a genial old man just leaving his farm door, and told him that we were literally dying for a drink of buttermilk. Our expression seemed to tickle him.

"Well!" he said, laughing, "it shall never be said that two poor creatures passed my door, and died for lack of a glass of buttermilk," and he brought out a huge jug, for which he would accept nothing but our blessings. He seemed to take buttermilk lightly; but, one evening, we came upon another old farmer to whom buttermilk seemed a species of the water of life to be hoarded jealously and doled out in careful quantities at strictly market rates.

In town one imagines that country people give their buttermilk to the pigs. At any rate, they didn't give it to us.

We paid that old man twenty cents, for we drank two glasses apiece. And first we had knocked at the farm door, and told our need to a pretty young woman, who answered, with some hesitancy, that she would call "father." She seemed to live in some awe of "father," as we well understood when a tall, raw-boned, stern, old man, of the caricature "Brother Jonathan" type, appeared grimly, making an iron sound with a great bunch of keys. On hearing our request, he said nothing, but, motioning to us to follow, stalked across the farmyard to a small building under a great elm-tree. There were two steps down to the door, and it had a mysterious appearance. It might have been a family vault, a dynamite magazine, or the Well at the World's End. It was the strong-room of the milk; and, when the grim old guardian of the dairy unlocked the door, with a sound of rusty locks and falling bolts, there, cool and cloistral, were the fragrant pans and bowls, the most sacred vessels of the farm.

> *"She bathed her body many a time*
> *In fountains filled with milk."*

I hummed to Colin; but I took care that the old man didn't hear me. And we agreed, as we went on again along the road, that he did right to guard well and charge well for so noble and so innocent a drink. Indeed, the old fellow's buttermilk was so good that I think it must have gone to my head. In no other way can I account for the following dithyrambic song:

> *Let whoso will sing Bacchus' vine,*
> *We know a drink that's more divine;*
>
> *'Tis white and innocent as doves,*
> *Fragrant and bosom-white as love's*
>
> *White bosom on a Summer day,*
> *And fragrant as the hawthorn spray.*
>
> *Let Dionysus and his crew,*

Garlanded, drain their fevered brew,
And in the orgiastic bowl
Drug and besot the sacred soul;

This simple country cup we drain
Knows not the ghosts of sin and pain,

No fates or furies follow him
Who sips from its cream-mantled rim.

Yea! all his thoughts are country-sweet,
And safe the walking of his feet,

However hard and long the way -
With country sleep to end the day.

To drain this cup no man shall rue -
The innocent madness of the dew

Who shall repent, or frenzy fine
Of morning star, or the divine

Inebriation of the hours
When May roofs in the world with flowers!

About this cup the swallows skim,
And the low milking-star hangs dim

Across the meadows, and the moon
Is near in heaven - the young moon;

And murmurs sweet of field and hill
Loiter awhile, and all is still.

As in some chapel dear to Pan,
The fair milk glimmers in the can,

And, in the silence cool and white,

The cream mounts through the listening night;

And, all around the sleeping house,
You hear the breathing of the cows,

And drowsy rattle of the chain,
Till lo! the blue-eyed morn again.

CHAPTER XIX

A GROWL ABOUT AMERICAN COUNTRY HOTELS

Though Colin and I had been walking but a very few days, after the first day or two it seemed as though we had been out on the road for weeks; as though, indeed, we had spent our lives in the open air; and it needed no more than our brief experience for us to realize what one so often reads of those who do actually live their lives out-of-doors, gypsies, sailors, cowboys and the like - how intolerable to them is a roof, and how literally they gasp for air and space in the confined walls of cities.

> Bed in the bush with stars to see,
> Bread I dip in the river -
>
> There's the life for a man like me,
> There's the life forever.

The only time of the day when our spirits began to fail was toward its close, when the shadows of supper and bed in some inclement inn began to fall over us, and we confessed to each other a positive sense of fear in our evening approach to the abodes of men. After a long, safe, care-free day, in the company of liberating prospects and sweet-breathed winds, there seemed a curious lurking menace in the most harmless village, as well as an unspeakable irksomeness in its inharmonious interruption of our mood. To emerge, saturated, body and soul, with the sweet scents and sounds and sights of a day's tramp, out of the meditative leafiness and spiritual temper of natural things, into the garishly lit street of some little provincial town, animated with the clumsy mirth of silly young country folks, aping so drearily the ribaldry, say, of Elmira, is a painful anticlimax to the spirit. Had it only been real Summer, instead of Indian Summer, we should, of course, have been real gypsies, and made our beds under the stars, but, as it was, we had no choice. Or, had we been walking in Europe ... yes, I am afraid the truth must out, and that our real dread at evening was - the American country hotel. With the best wish in the world, it is impossible to be enthusiastic over the American country hotel. How ironically the kindly old words used to come floating to me out of Shakespeare each evening as the shadows fell, and the lights came out in the windows - "to take mine ease at mine inn;" and assuredly it was on another planet that Shenstone wrote:

Whoe'er hath travelled life's dull round,
Whate'er his fortunes may have been,
Must sigh to think he still has found
His warmest welcome at an inn.

Had Shenstone been writing in an American country hotel, his tune would probably have been more after this fashion: "A wonderful day has come to a dreary end in the most sepulchral of hotels, a mouldy, barn-like place, ill-lit, mildewed and unspeakably dismal. A comfortless room with two beds and two low-power electric lights, two stiff chairs, an uncompanionable sofa, and some ghastly pictures of simpering naked women. We have bought some candles, and made a candlestick out of a soap-dish. Colin is making the best of it with 'The Beloved Vagabond,' and I have drawn up one of the chairs to a table with a mottled marble top, and am writing this amid a gloom which you could cut with a knife, and which is so perfect of its kind as to be almost laughable. But for the mail, which we found with unutterable thankfulness at the post-office, I hardly dare think what would have happened to us, to what desperate extremities we might not have been driven, though even the possibilities of despair seem limited in this second-hand tomb of a town...."

Here Colin looks up with a wry smile and ironically quotes from the wisdom of Paragot: "What does it matter where the body finds itself, so long as the soul has its serene habitations?" This wail is too typical of most of our hotel experiences. As a rule we found the humble, cheaper hotels best, and, whenever we had a choice of two, chose the less pretentious.

Sometimes as, on entering a town or village, we asked some passer-by about the hotels, we would be looked over and somewhat doubtfully asked: "Do you want a two-dollar house?" And we soon learned to pocket òur pride, and ask if there was not a cheaper house. Strange that people whose business is hospitality should be so inhospitable, and strange that the American travelling salesman, a companionable creature, not averse from comfort, should not have created a better condition of things. For the inn should be the natural harmonious close to the day, as much a part of the day's music as the setting sun. It should be the gratefully sought shelter from the homeless night, the sympathetic friend of hungry stomachs and dusty feet, the cozy jingle of social pipes and dreamy after-dinner talk, the abode of snowy beds for luxuriously aching limbs, lavendered sheets and pleasant dreams.

But, as people without any humour usually say, "A sense of humour helps under all circumstances"; and we managed to extract a great deal of fun out of the rigours of the American country hotel.

In one particularly inhospitable home of hospitality, for example, we found no little consolation from the directions printed over the very simple and familiar device for calling up the hotel desk. The device was nothing more remarkable than the button of an ordinary electric bell, which you were, in the usual way, to push once for bell-boy, twice for ice-water, three times for chambermaid, and so on. However, the hotel evidently regarded it as one of the marvels of advanced science and referred to it, in solemnly printed "rules" for its use, as no less than "The Emergency Drop Annunciator!" Angels of the

Annunciation! what a heavenly phrase!

But this is an ill-tempered chapter - let us begin another.

CHAPTER XX

ONIONS, PIGS AND HICKORY-NUTS

One feature of the countryside in which from time to time we found innocent amusement was the blackboards placed outside farmhouses, on which are written, that is, "annunciated," the various products the farmer has for sale, such as apples, potatoes, honey, and so forth. On one occasion we read: "Get your horses' teeth floated here." There was no one to ask about what this mysterious proclamation meant. No doubt it was clear as daylight to the neighbours, but to us it still remains a mystery. Perhaps the reader knows what it meant. Then on another occasion we read: "Onions and Pigs For Sale." Why this curious collocation of onions and pigs? Colin suggested that, of course, the onions were to stuff the pigs with.

"And here's an idea," he continued. "Suppose we go in and buy a little suckling-pig and a string of onions. Then we will buy a yard of two of blue ribbon and tie it round the pig's neck, and you shall lead it along the road, weeping. I will walk behind it, with the onions, grinning from ear to ear. And when any one meets us, and asks the meaning of the strange procession, you will say: 'I am weeping because our little pig has to die!' And if any one says to me, 'Why are you grinning from ear to ear?' I shall answer, 'Because I am going to eat him. We are going to stuff him with onions at the next inn, and eat roast pig at the rising of the moon.'"

But we lacked courage to put our little joke into practice, fearing an insufficient appreciation of the fantastic in that particular region.

We were now making for Watkins, and had spent the night at Bradford, a particularly charming village almost lost amid the wooded hills of another lovely and spacious valley, through which we had lyrically walked the day before. Bradford is a real country village, and was already all in a darkness smelling of cows and apples, when we groped for it among the woods the evening before. At starting out next morning, we inquired the way to Watkins of a storekeeper standing at his shop-door. He was in conversation with an acquaintance, and our questions occasioned a lively argument as to which was the better of two roads. The acquaintance was for the road through "Pine Creek," and he added, with a grim smile, "I guess I should know; I've travelled it often enough with a heavy load behind"; and the recollection of the rough hills he had gone bumping over, all evidently fresh in his mind, seemed to give him a curious amusement. It transpired that he was an undertaker!

So we took the road to Pine Creek, but at the threshold of the village our fancy was taken by the particularly quaint white wooden meeting-house, surrounded on three sides with tie-up sheds for vehicles, each stall having a name affixed to it, like a pew: "P. Yawger," "A.W. Gillum," "Pastor," and so on. Here the pious of the district tied up their buggies while they went within to pray, and these sacred stalls made a quaint picture for the imagination of outlying farmers driving to meeting over the hills on Sabbath mornings.

It was a beautiful morning of veiled sunshine, so warm that some hardy crickets chirped faintly as we went along. Once a blue jay came and looked at us, and the squirrels whirred among the chestnuts and hickories, and the roadsides were so thickly strewn with fallen nuts that we made but slow progress, stopping all the time to fill our pockets.

For a full hour we sat down with a couple of stones for nut-crackers, and forgot each other and everything else in the hypnotizing occupation of cracking hickory-nuts. And we told each other that thus do grown sad men become boys again, by a woodside, of an October morning, cracking hickory-nuts, the world well lost.

RICHARD LE GALLIENNE

CHAPTER XXI

OCTOBER ROSES AND A YOUNG GIRL'S FACE

The undertaker was certainly right about the road. I think he must have had a flash of poetic insight into our taste in roads. This was not, as a rule, understood by the friendly country folk. Their ideas and ours as to what constituted a good road differed beyond the possibility of harmonizing. When they said that a road was good they meant that it was straight, level, and businesslike. When they said that a road was bad they meant that it was rugged, rambling and picturesque. So, to their bewilderment, whenever we had a choice of good or bad roads, we always chose the bad. And, to get at what we really wanted, we learned to inquire which was the worst road to such and such a place. That we knew would be the road for us. From their point of view, the road we were on was as bad as could be; but, as I said, the undertaker evidently understood us, and had sent us into a region of whimsically sudden hills and rock and wooded wilderness, a swart country of lonely, rugged uplands, with but a solitary house here and there for miles. It was resting at the top of one of these hard-won acclivities that we came upon - and remember that it was the middle of October - two wild roses blooming by the roadside. This seems a fact worthy the attention of botanical societies, and I still have the roses pressed for the inspection of the learned between the pages of my travelling copy of Hans Andersen's "Fairy Tales."

A fact additionally curious was that the bush on which the flowers grew seemed to be the only rose-bush in the region.

We looked about us in vain to find another. How had that single rose-bush come to be, an uncompanioned exotic, in the rough society of pines and oaks and hickories, on a rocky hill-top swept by the North wind, and how had those frail, scented petals found strength and courage thus to bloom alone in the doorway of Winter? And, why, out of all the roses of the world, had these two been chosen, still, so late in the year, to hold up the tattered standard of Summer?

Why, in the empty Autumn woods,
And all the loss and end of things,
Does one leaf linger on the tree;
Why is it only one bird sings?

And why, across the aching field,
Does one lone cricket chirrup on;
Why one surviving butterfly,
With all its bright companions gone?

And why, when faces all about
Whiten and wither hour by hour,
Does one old face bloom on so sweet,
As young as when it was a flower?

The same mystery was again presented to us a little farther along the road, as we stopped at a lone schoolhouse among the hills, the only house to be seen, and asked our way of the young schoolmarm. The door had been left half open, and, knocking, we had stepped into the almost empty schoolroom, with its portrait of Lincoln and a map of the United States. Three scholars sat there with their kindly-faced teacher, studying geography amid the silence of the hills, which the little room seemed to concentrate in a murmuring hush, like a shell. A little boy sat by himself a desk or two behind two young girls, and as we entered, and the studious faces looked up in surprise, we saw only the pure brows and the great spiritual eyes of the older girl, almost a woman, and we thought of the lonely roses we had found up on the hillside.

Here was another rose blooming in the wilderness, a face lovely and beautiful as a spring reflecting the sky in the middle of a wood. How had she come there, that beautiful child-woman in the solitude? By what caprice of the strange law of the distribution of fair faces had she come to flower in this particular waste place of the earth? - for her face had surely come a long way, been blown blossom-wise on some far wandering wind, from realms of old beauty and romance, and it had the exiled look of all beautiful things. Could she be a plain farmer's daughter, indigenous to that stubborn soil? No, surely she was not that, and yet - how had she come to be there? But these were questions we could not put to the schoolmarm. We could only ask our road, and the prosaic possibilities of lunch in the neighbourhood, and go on our way. Nor could I press that rose among the pages of my book - but, as I write, I wonder if it is still making sweet that desolate spot, and still studying irrelevant geography in the silence of the hills.

However, we did learn something about our young human rose at a farmhouse a mile or so farther on. While a motherly housewife prepared us some lunch, all a-bustle with expectancy of an imminent inroad of harvesters due to thresh the corn, and liable to eat all before them, a sprightly young daughter, who attended the same school, and whom we had told about our call at the schoolhouse, entertained us with girlish gossip of the neighbourhood. So we learned that our fancies had not been so far wrong, but that our beautiful young face had indeed come from as far as France, the orphaned child of a French sailor and an English mother, come over the seas for a home with a farmer uncle near by. Strange are the destinies of beautiful faces. All the way from France to Pine Creek! Poor little world-wandered rose!

And while we ate our lunch, the mother had a sad, beautiful story of a dead son and a mother's tears to tell us, too sacred to tell again. How many beautiful faces there are hidden about the world, and how many beautiful sad stories hidden in the broken hearts of mothers!

CHAPTER XXII

CONCERNING THE POPULAR TASTE IN SCENERY AND SOME HAPPY PEOPLE

We had somewhat scorned the idea of Watkins, as being one of Nature's show-places. In fact, Watkins Glen is, so to say, so nationally beautiful as latterly to have received a pension from the Government of the United States, which now undertakes the conservation of its fantastic chasms and waterfalls. Some one - I am inclined to think it was myself - once said that he never wished to go to Switzerland, because he feared that the Alps would be greasy with being climbed. I think it is clear what he meant. To one who loves Nature for himself, has his own discovering eyes for her multiform and many-mooded beauty, it is distasteful to have some excursionist effect of spectacular scenery labelled and thrust upon him with a showman's raptures; and, in revulsion from the hypocritical admiration of the vulgar, he turns to the less obvious and less melodramatic beauty of the natural world. The common eye can see Nature's beauty only in such melodramatic and sentimental forms - dizzy chasms, foaming waterfalls, snow-capped mountains and flagrant sunsets, just as it can realize Nature's wildness of heart only in a menagerie. That a squirrel or a meadow-lark, or even a guinea-pig, is just as wild as the wild beasts in a travelling circus is outside the comprehension of the vulgar, who really hunger after mere marvels, whatever they may be, and actually have no eyes for beauty at all.

Thus really sublime and grandiose effects of Nature are apt to lose their edge for us by over-popularization, as many of her

RICHARD LE GALLIENNE

scenes and moods have come to seem platitude from being over-painted. Niagara has suffered far more from the sentimental tourist and the landscape artist than from all the power-houses, and one has to make a strenuous effort of detachment from its excursionist associations to appreciate its sublimity.

Thus Colin and I discussed, in a somewhat bored way, whether we should trouble to visit the famous Watkins Glen, as we sat over supper in a Watkins hotel, one of the few really comfortable and cordial hotels we met in our wanderings, and we smiled to think what the natives would have made of our conversation. Two professional lovers of beauty calmly discussing whether it was worth while walking half a mile to see one of the natural, and national, wonders of America! Why, last season more than half a million visitors kodaked it, and wrote their names on the face of the rocks! However, a great natural effect holds its own against no little vulgarization, and Watkins Glen soon made us forget the trippers and the concrete footpaths and iron railings of the United States government, in the fantasies of its weirdly channelled gorge and mysterious busy water.

Watkins itself, despite its name, is sufficiently favoured by Nature to make an easy annual living, situated as it is at the south end of the beautiful Seneca Lake, and at the head of a nobly picturesque valley some twenty miles long, with a pretty river spreading out into flashing reed-grown flats, sheer cliffs and minor waterfalls, here and there a vineyard on the hillside, or the vivid green of celery trenches in the dark loam of the hollows, all the way to - Elmira! The river and the trolley run side by side the whole charming way, and, as you near Elmira, you come upon latticed barns that waft you the fragrance of drying tobacco-leaves, suspended longitudinally for the wind to play through. On the morning of our leaving Watkins, we had been roused a little earlier than usual by mirthful sounds in the street beneath our hotel windows. Light-hearted voices joking each other floated up to us, and some one out of the gladness of his heart was executing a spirited shake-down on the sidewalk - at six o'clock of a misty October morning. Looking out, we caught an endearing glimpse of the life of the most lovable of all professions. It was a theatrical company that had played a one-night stand at the local opera-house the evening before, and was now once more upon its wandering way. They had certainly been up till past midnight, but here they were, at six o'clock of the morning, merry as larks, gay as children, waiting for the Elmira trolley. Presently the car came clanging up, and alongside drew up a big float, containing baggage and rolls of scenery - all of which, to our astonishment, by some miracle of loading known only to baggagemen, was in a few moments stowed away into the waiting car. When the last property was shipped, the conductor rang his bell, by way of warning, and the whole group, like a flight of happy birds, climbed chattering into the car. "All aboard," called the conductor, once more ringing his bell, and off they went, leaving a trail of laughter in the morning air.

"'Beloved Vagabonds!'" said Colin, as we turned away, lonely, from our windows, with, I hardly know why, a suspicion of tears in our eyes.

RICHARD LE GALLIENNE

CHAPTER XXIII

THE SUSQUEHANNA

Here for a while a shadow seemed to fall over our trip. No doubt it was the shadow of the great town we were approaching. Not that we have anything against Elmira, though possibly its embattled reformatory, frowning from the hillside, contributed its gloomy associations to our spirits. It was against towns in general that our gorge rose. Did our vagabond ethics necessitate our conscientiously tramping every foot of these "gritty paving-stones," we asked each other, as we entered upon a region of depressing suburbs, and we called a halt on the spot to discuss the point. The discussion was not long, and it was brought to a cheerful, demoralized end by the approach of the trolley, into which, regardless of right or wrong, we climbed with alacrity, not to alight till not only Elmira was left behind, but more weary suburbs, too, on the other side. That night, as old travellers phrase it, we lay at Waverly, on the frontier of Pennsylvania, a sad, dirty little town, grotesquely belying its romantic name, and only surpassed in squalor by the classically named Athens - beware, reader, of American towns named out of classical dictionaries! Here, however, our wanderings in the brick-and-mortar wilderness were to end, for by a long, romantic, old, covered bridge we crossed the Chemung River, and there once more, on the other side, was Nature, lovelier than ever, awaiting us. Not Dante, when he emerged from Hades and again beheld the stars, drew deeper breaths of escape than we, thus escaping from - Athens!

And soon we were to meet the Susquehanna - beautiful, broad-bosomed name, that has always haunted my imagination like the name of some beautiful savage princess - *La belle sauvage.* Susquehanna! What a southern opulence in the soft, seductive syllables! Yes, soon we were to meet the Susquehanna. Nor had we long to wait, and little did we suspect what our meeting with that beautiful river was to mean.

The Chemung, on whose east bank we were now walking, seemed a noble enough river, very broad and all the more picturesque for being shallow with the Summer drought; and its shining reaches and wooded banks lifted up our hearts. She, like ourselves, was on her way to join the Susquehanna, a mile or two below, and we said to ourselves, that, beautiful as the land had been through which we had already passed, we were now entering on a Nature of more heroic mould, mightier contours, and larger aspects. We were henceforth to walk in the company of great rivers: the Susquehanna, like some epic goddess, was to lead us to the Lehigh; the Blue Mountains were to bring us to the Delaware; and the uplands of Sullivan County were to bring us to - the lordly gates of the Hudson.

Our chests expanded as imagination luxuriated in the pictures it made. Our walk was only just beginning.

RICHARD LE GALLIENNE

CHAPTER XXIV

AND UNEXPECTEDLY THE LAST

We had seen the two great rivers sweep into each other's arms in a broad glory of sunlit water, meeting at the bosky end of a wooded promontory, and yes! there was the Susquehanna glittering far beneath - the beautiful name I had so often seen and wondered about, painted on the sides of giant freight-cars! Yes, there was actually the great legendary river. It was a very warm, almost sultry noonday, more like midsummer than mid-October, and the river was almost blinding in its flashing beauty. Loosening our knapsacks, we called a halt and, leaning over the railing guarding the precipitous bank, luxuriated in the visionary scene. So high was the bank, and so broad the river, that we seemed lifted up into space, and the river, dreamily flowing beneath a gauze veil of heat-mist, seemed miles below us and drowsily unreal. Its course inshore was dotted with boulders, in the shadows of which we could see long ghostly fishes lazily gliding, and a mud-turtle, with a trail of little ones, slowly moving from rock to rock.

Suddenly Colin put his hand to his head, and swayed toward me, as though he were about to faint.

"I don't know what's the matter, old man," he said, "but I think I had better sit down a minute." And he sank by the roadside.

Unlike himself, he had been complaining of fatigue, and had seemed out of sorts for a day or two, but we had thought nothing of it; and, after resting a few minutes, he announced himself ready for the road again, but he looked very pale and walked with evident weariness. As a roadside cottage came in sight, "I wonder if they could give us a cup of tea," he said; "that would fix me up, I'm sure." So we knocked, and the door was opened by a pathetic shadow of an old woman, very poor and thin and weary-looking, who, although, as we presently learned, she was at the moment suffering from the recent loss of one eye, made us welcome and busied herself about tea, with an unselfish kindness that touched our hearts, and made us reflect on the angelic goodness of human nature - sometimes.

She looked anxiously, mother-like, at Colin, and persuaded him to lie down and rest awhile in her little parlour, and, while he rested, she and I talked and she told me how she had come by her blind eye - an odd, harmless-sounding cause. She had been looking up into one of her apple-trees, one day, a few weeks ago, and an apple had fallen and struck her in the eye. Such innocent means does Nature sometimes use for her cruel accidents of disease and death! Just an apple falling from a tree, - and you are blind! A fly stings you, on a Summer day, and you die.

Colin, rested and refreshed, we once more started on our way, but, bravely as he strode on, there was no disguising it - my blithe, happy-hearted companion was ill. Of course we both assured the other that it could be nothing, but privately our hearts sank with a vague fear we did not speak. At length, after a weary four miles, we reached Towanda.

"I'm afraid," said poor Colin, "I can walk no more to-day. Perhaps a good night's rest will make me all right." We found an inn, and while Colin threw himself, wearied, on his bed, I went out, not telling him, and sought a doctor.

"And you've been walking with this temperature?" said the learned man, when he had seated himself at Colin's bedside and felt his wrist. "Have you been drinking much water

RICHARD LE GALLIENNE

as you went along? ... H'm - it's been a very dry Summer, you know."

And the words of our friend in the buggy came back to us with sickening emphasis. O those innocent-looking fairy wells and magic mirrors by the road-side! And I thought, too, of the poor old blinded woman and the falling apple. Was Nature really like that?

And then the wise man's verdict fell on our ears like a doom.

"Take my advice, and don't walk any more, but catch the night train for New York."

Poor Colin! But there was no appeal.

The end of our trip had come, suddenly, unreasonably, stupidly, like this.

"So we've got to be shot into New York like a package through a tube, after all!' said Colin. "No lordly gates of the Hudson for us! What a fool I feel, to be the one to spoil our trip like this!"

And the tears glistened in our eyes, as we pressed each other's hand in that dreary iron bedroom, with the shadow of we knew not what for Colin over us - for our comradeship had been very good, day by day, together on the open road.

Our train did not go till midnight, so we had a long melancholy evening before us; but the doctor had given Colin some mysterious potion containing rest, and presently, as I sat by his side in the gray twilight, he fell into a deep sleep - a sleep, alas! of fire and wandering talk. It was pitiful to hear him, poor fellow - living over again in dreams the road we had travelled, or making pictures of the road he still dreamed ahead of us. Never before had I realized how entirely his soul was the soul of a painter - all pictures and colour.

"O my God!" he would suddenly exclaim, "did you ever see such blue in your life!" and then again, evidently referring to some particularly attractive effect in the phantasmagoria of his fever, "it's no use - you must let me stop and have a shot to get that, before it goes."

One place that seemed particularly to haunt him was - Mauch Chunk. He had been there before, and, as we had walked along, had often talked enthusiastically of it. "Wait till we get to Mauch Chunk," he said; "then the real fun will begin." And now, over and over again, he kept making pictures of Mauch Chunk, till I could have cried.

"Dramatic black rocks," he would murmur, "water rushing from the hills in every direction - clean-cut, vivid scenery - like theatres - the road runs by the side of a steel-blue river at the bottom of a chasm, and there is hardly room for it - the houses cling to the hillside like swallows' nests - here and there patches of fresh green grass gleam among the rocks, and, high up in the air on some dizzy ledge, there is a wild apple-tree in blossom - it is all black rocks and springs and moss and tumbling water -"

Then again his soul was evidently walking in the Blue Mountains, and several times he repeated a phrase of mine that had taken his fancy: "And now for the spacious corridors of the Highlands, and the lordly gates of the Hudson."

Then he would suddenly half awaken and turn to me, realizing the truth, and say:

"O our beautiful journey - to end like this!" and fall asleep again.

And once more I fell to thinking of fairy springs by the roadside, and apples falling innocently from the bough, and how the beautiful journey we call life might some day suddenly end like this, with half the beautiful road untravelled - the rest sleep and perchance dreams.

RICHARD LE GALLIENNE

* * * * *

But Colin did not die. He is once more painting out in the sun, and next year we plan to stand again on that very spot by the Susquehanna, and watch the shadows of great fishes gliding through the dreamy water, and the mud-turtle with her trail of little ones moving from rock to rock - and then we shall strike out on the road again, just where we left off that October afternoon; but the reader need not be afraid - we shall not write a book about it.

ENVOI

And now the merry way we took
Is nothing but a printed book;

We would you had been really there,
Out with us in the open air -

For, after all, the best of words
Are but a poor exchange for birds.

Yet if, perchance, this book of ours
Should sometimes make you think of flowers,

Orchards and barns and harvest wain,
"It was not written all in vain -"

So authors used to make their bow,
As, Gentle Reader, we do now.

Choose from Thousands of 1stWorldLibrary Classics By

Adolphus WilliamWard
Aesop
Agatha Christie
Alexander Aaronsohn
Alexander Kielland
Alexandre Dumas
Alfred Gatty
Alfred Ollivant
Alice Duer Miller
Alice Turner Curtis
Alice Dunbar
Ambrose Bierce
Amelia E. Barr
Andrew Lang
Andrew McFarland Davis
Anna Sewell
Annie Besant
Annie Hamilton Donnell
Annie Payson Call
Anton Chekhov
Arnold Bennett
Arthur Conan Doyle
Arthur Ransome
Atticus
B. M. Bower
Basil King
Bayard Taylor
Ben Macomber
Booth Tarkington
Bram Stoker
C. Collodi
C. E. Orr
C. M. Ingleby
Carolyn Wells
Catherine Parr Traill
Charles A. Eastman
Charles Dickens
Charles Dudley Warner
Charles Farrar Browne
Charles Ives
Charles Kingsley
Charles Lathrop Pack
Charles Whibley
Charles Willing Beale
Charlotte M. Braeme
Charlotte M.Yonge
Clair W. Hayes
Clarence Day Jr.
Clarence E. Mulford

Clemence Housman
Confucius
Cornelis DeWitt Wilcox
Cyril Burleigh
D. H. Lawrence
Daniel Defoe
David Garnett
Don Carlos Janes
Donald Keyhole
Dorothy Kilner
Dougan Clark
E. Nesbit
E.P.Roe
E. Phillips Oppenheim
Edgar Allan Poe
Edgar Rice Burroughs
Edith Wharton
Edward J. O'Biren
John Cournos
Edwin L. Arnold
Eleanor Atkins
Elizabeth Cleghorn
Gaskell
Elizabeth Von Arnim
Ellem Key
Emily Dickinson
Erasmus W. Jones
Ernie Howard Pie
Ethel Turner
Ethel Watts Mumford
Eugenie Foa
Eugene Wood
Evelyn Everett-Green
Everard Cotes
F. J. Cross
Federick Austin Ogg
Ferdinand Ossendowski
Francis Bacon
Francis Darwin
Frances Hodgson Burnett
Frank Gee Patchin
Frank Harris
Frank Jewett Mather
Frank L. Packard
Frederick Trevor Hill
Frederick Winslow Taylor
Friedrich Kerst
Friedrich Nietzsche
Fyodor Dostoyevsky

Gabrielle E. Jackson
Garrett P. Serviss
Gaston Leroux
George Ade
Geroge Bernard Shaw
George Ebers
George Eliot
George MacDonald
George Orwell
George Tucker
George W. Cable
George Wharton James
Gertrude Atherton
Grace E. King
Grant Allen
Guillermo A. Sherwell
Gulielma Zollinger
Gustav Flaubert
H. A. Cody
H. B. Irving
H. G. Wells
H. H. Munro
H. Irving Hancock
H. Rider Haggard
H. W. C. Davis
Hamilton Wright Mabie
Hans Christian Andersen
Harold Avery
Harold McGrath
Harriet Beecher Stowe
Harry Houidini
Helent Hunt Jackson
Helen Nicolay
Hendy David Thoreau
Henrik Ibsen
Henry Adams
Henry Ford
Henry Frost
Henry James
Henry Jones Ford
Henry Seton Merriman
Henry Wadsworth
Longfellow
Henry W Longfellow
Herbert A. Giles
Herbert N. Casson
Herman Hesse
Homer
Honore De Balzac

Horace Walpole
Horatio Alger, Jr.
Howard Pyle
Howard R. Garis
Hugh Lofting
Hugh Walpole
Humphry Ward
Ian Maclaren
Israel Abrahams
J.G.Austin
J. Henri Fabre
J. M. Barrie
J. Macdonald Oxley
J. S. Knowles
J. Storer Clouston
Jack London
Jacob Abbott
James Allen
James Lane Allen
James Andrews
James Baldwin
James DeMille
James Joyce
James Oliver Curwood
James Oppenheim
James Otis
Jane Austen
Jens Peter Jacobsen
Jerome K. Jerome
John Burroughs
John F. Kennedy
John Gay
John Glasworthy
John Habberton
John Joy Bell
John Milton
John Philip Sousa
Jonathan Swift
Joseph Carey
Joseph Conrad
Joseph Jacobs
Julian Hawthrone
Julies Vernes
Justin Huntly McCarthy
Kakuzo Okakura
Kenneth Grahame
Kate Langley Bosher
L. A. Abbot
L. T. Meade
L. Frank Baum
Laura Lee Hope

Laurence Housman
Leo Tolstoy
Leonid Andreyev
Lewis Carroll
Lilian Bell
Lloyd Osbourne
Louis Tracy
Louisa May Alcott
Lucy Fitch Perkins
Lucy Maud Montgomery
Lydia Miller Middleton
Lyndon Orr
M. H. Adams
Margaret E. Sangster
Margaret Vandercook
Maria Edgeworth
Maria Thompson Daviess
Mariano Azuela
Marion Polk Angellotti
Mark Overton
Mark Twain
Mary Austin
Mary Cole
Mary Rowlandson
Mary Wollstonecraft
Shelley
Max Beerbohm
Myra Kelly
Nathaniel Hawthrone
O. F. Walton
Oscar Wilde
Owen Johnson
P.G.Wodehouse
Paul and Mable Thorn
Paul G. Tomlinson
Paul Severing
Peter B. Kyne
Plato
R. Derby Holmes
R. L. Stevenson
Rabindranath Tagore
Rahul Alvares
Ralph Waldo Emmerson
Rene Descartes
Rex E. Beach
Richard Harding Davis
Richard Jefferies
Robert Barr
Robert Frost
Robert Gordon Anderson
Robert L. Drake

Robert Lansing
Robert Michael Ballantyne
Robert W. Chambers
Rosa Nouchette Carey
Ross Kay
Rudyard Kipling
Samuel B. Allison
Samuel Hopkins Adams
Sarah Bernhardt
Selma Lagerlof
Sherwood Anderson
Sigmund Freud
Standish O'Grady
Stanley Weyman
Stella Benson
Stephen Crane
Stewart Edward White
Stijn Streuvels
Swami Abhedananda
Swami Parmananda
T. S. Ackland
The Princess Der Ling
Thomas A. Janvier
Thomas A Kempis
Thomas Anderton
Thomas Bailey Aldrich
Thomas Bulfinch
Thomas De Quincey
Thomas H. Huxley
Thomas Hardy
Thomas More
Thornton W. Burgess
U. S. Grant
Valentine Williams
Victor Appleton
Virginia Woolf
Walter Scott
Washington Irving
Wilbur Lawton
Wilkie Collins
Willa Cather
Willard F. Baker
William Makepeace
Thackeray
William W. Walter
Winston Churchill
Yei Theodora Ozaki
Young E. Allison
Zane Grey